MW01110237

To PETER
BEST WISHES
Giovanni Chorea
2016

Clones
Aliens or Us?

Giovanni Rocca

MR Comics & Art • Andover, Massachusetts

MR Comics & Art
5 Binney Street, Andover, MA 01810

Published 2010

ISBN 978-1-4507-0779-4

Book design by Kevin A. Wilson
Upper Case Textual Services

Cover art by Giovanni Rocca

What is it? What does it mean?
The answer is inside!

1?

Prologue

A strange experience. It seems like everyone who has had contact with these Strangers says the same thing, and they see the same thing. It is very hard to explain what it is they see, or they think they see. It is hard to understand because the information is not really true; it is bogus. It looks like it comes from a science fiction book. We have a lot of science fiction books on this topic, but what we think we know is completely off target. Some people talk about this like they know what they are talking about; they are convinced that we don't live in this world alone, and those convinced of this extraterrestrial imagination and illusion also think that the universe is populated with different creatures than we humans. So some of these people came to the conclusion that these creatures have a specific look, and in these descriptions the aliens have a particular look. People believe that they know what they look like. They describe them as being small in stature, approximately three feet tall; they are skinny, with long arms and fingers, small feet, big heads and big eyes, with two small holes for a nose, almost no mouth, and tiny ears. They don't speak, but they can communicate with the whole world, or at least people claim to have witnessed this phenomenon all over the world. But more encounters with aliens seem to happen in America than any other part of the world. We don't know why, but it is becoming very complicated and, at times, very confusing.

We have no proof whatsoever that these creatures exist, no proof that they came to our world. No trace of any gases or radioactive materials has been found on the ground, in the air, or in plants. There is no trace of any foreign substance or any kind of electric current in any of these people who claim they were abducted. Doctors and scientists assert that these so-called abductions are really an illusion or a fanatic dream. We often come up with our own theories just to have conversations with each other. Personally, I believe that someone had a dream, and with this dream he invented a story. He sketched what he thought he saw in his dreams, and that was how the aliens came about. Having seen the picture, it stayed in our mind, persuading some to believe that it is true. When they talk about this matter, it is true, or at least they believe it to be. They are not lying. To them these experiences are clear. They know without having proof. If it were true, if the aliens had the capabilities people claim, imagine what they could do to us and the world. In all probability, the world would be destroyed. Because of their superiority, there would be no competition. The human race would have no chance to save itself. We know by these people's accounts of these abductions that the aliens have an enormous intelligence, the capacity to fly at the speed of light, and the abililty to take anyone they want whenever they want.

The abducted will return in very short time. The power

of these aliens is almost impossible for the human race to understand, even today in this age of science, computers, and advanced technology. The human race is investing a great deal of money and time to make contact with these aliens from another planet. So far, we have had no answer, no contact with anything out there in the universe. We are consuming time and money just to build gigantic telescopic lenses and satellites, and sending all kind of equipment out to space in the hope of finding any small piece of information or any type of contact. So far we have nothing to show for our time and effort. Why? Because beyond the planet earth, no sentient creatures or advanced civilizations exist. We are alone.

Even with all these books, all this information, we still don't have proof of alien life, and our knowledge of UFOs is limited. All these books are there to read and expand your way of thinking, but all these books are there for your imagination and to pass time. Eventually each person comes to their own conclusion. It is like a game for our own amusement. With a little study, you can come to some understanding of what you read, because books are nothing but tools, stories that allow the human race to advance in medicine, architecture, geography, music, and art, and to improve the quality of our lives. Because without science we can't come to an understanding of UFO matters and the stories people tell about them. It can be dangerous when we don't have enough data because imagination grows, and there is no limitation on how far we can go with science fiction stories and fables, even to the point of us becoming mixed up between science-fiction and reality, not being able to distinguish fact from fiction. Imagination can drive man into danger, especially with regards to mental health.

This book I am writing is just imagination. I am doing this not because I believe, but because I want to give you a vision of one possible future. I am saying that it can happen, not that it will happen. Even in this book, imagination is strong. In my studies I discovered that a man without imagination is limited. I believe in a lot of things, but I also don't believe in a lot of things. Because of this I am writing this book of imagination of UFOs and Strangers. In my mind, these Strangers are nothing but us. To understand this we need to think like a dream, because I myself have no proof what I am writing. Belief without proof is in vain, but without our imagination we have no writing

The story begins like this.

Chapter One

Space, a vast area of darkness, with tiny little dots of light coming from the right. In an instant, the darkness is filled with these dots from every part of the universe. From a distance, a speck of light is moving toward the earth at the speed of light, passing through galaxy after galaxy. Reaching our own galaxy, passing planets that we don't even recognize. Passing by our own planets, Neptune, Uranus, Jupiter, and the other planets, straight toward Earth. Penetrating our own atmosphere and passing through the clouds. This begins in the future. The events take place in the south of Italy, in the region of Calabria.

I was resting next to a fig tree, one of my favorite spots to relax after a long day of working on my farm. The sky was beautiful and clear, with a full moon visible, and you could still see some of the sun on the horizon. I almost was sleeping but not quite asleep, when suddenly I saw a very brilliant light. It was so bright that it lit the whole sky, making it look more like midday than the early evening. The trees around me were illuminated. I felt a tremor from the earth. I learned later that this same scenario occurred in Africa, China, North and South America, and all parts of the world, all at the same time. But for some reason I was the only one who was given proof, proof I am to share with scientists and world leaders.

I could not understand what was going on. I was seeing things. I saw this bright light, so strong that I couldn't understand what it was. Then I saw other lights shining with all different colors, including some colors I had never seen before. These lights looked to me as though they were from another world. They seemed to be there to calm me down, to relax my eyes, to make me comfortable, physically and mentally. For a second I felt as though I was in heaven. I was not afraid. For some reason, I trusted the whole situation, even though I felt paralyzed. I couldn't move or speak; I could only hear and see.

I suddenly realized that there was someone standing before me. I saw a form that was almost human, but with slight differences. It looked like pictures I had seen in books on UFOs and images in movies. He had a small body, a large head, and big black eyes that seemed to be entirely composed of pupil. He had two small holes for a nose and tiny ears. For a moment it seemed like what I had read and heard and seen on TV about aliens were true. But when I saw this particular figure, I thought, "My god, it is true! Everything I didn't believe is now standing right in front of me! Now I am in their situation. What do I do? What will they do to me?" I was paralyzed, on the ground. I couldn't run or scream. I could only wait to see what would happen next.

The figure was walking toward me. He was pacing, but at the same time not pacing. It looked as though he were walking, but in reality he was elevated from the ground about thirty centimeters. The closer he came the more his shape seemed to change. It looked to me as if he were growing. I looked up and saw his head, which was about the proportion of a human head. The body was also roughly proportional to that of a human. Suddenly, it dawned on me that this figure was nothing like what I read or heard or saw on TV or movies. This alien was not what I suspected. It was so close to me, yet I was not scared of the strange figure. The Stranger did not speak to me. He came closer and closer to me to the point that I could clearly see his appearance. His body was shining like chrome. His hands were empty with no guns, instruments, or any kind of weapons. The Stranger was close to me, about one meter away. I saw the eyes of the figure. The eyes were blue, but they were not regular eyes, like a light across the face, from ear to ear. He appeared to be bald. The body looked like it was covered with this chrome, metallic material. I couldn't see the face. I didn't notice a nose, mouth, or even ears. When I looked at the figure, I stood up, and I looked up, because the figure was so tall. I estimated his height to be over two meters. He was much taller than I was, and I am one meter eighty centimeters. The figure remained with me for about thirty seconds, just standing in front of me.

A short distance away, I saw another figure walking toward me, looking exactly like the first one. Then I saw a third figure just like the first two. They were very close to me, all three of them. They seemed to be communicating with each other, but I couldn't hear anything. I didn't hear any sound or feel any vibration. All the brilliance from the light remained the same. Nothing changed for a while, but suddenly everything started shaking. There was a tremendous tremor, so strong that I was shaking. The figures, however, remained motionless. Although I felt I was in a dream, the figures were so real and believable that I knew it was reality. The first figure closest to me put an arm on my shoulder and began to speak to me telepathically.

Chapter Two

The Stranger approached me. "Don't be afraid. I am a friend. I will not harm you."

"I am not afraid," I replied, "but I am confused."

"I know," the Stranger said, reassuringly. "I will explain."

"When?"

"In a few minutes. Everything will be clear to you then."

I closed my eyes for a moment, and then looked up at the Stranger. "Please, if it is possible, I would like to know how you can speak my language."

"Your language is my language," the Stranger answered, "as are all other languages."

"I need to go home," I said. "It is very late. My family is waiting for me for dinner."

"Don't worry," the Stranger said, once again in a reassuring tone. "Your family is alright."

"What are you going to do with me?"

"Nothing bad. You will see."

I was by no means certain. "Are you going to take me away from the earth?"

"Don't worry," the Stranger repeated. "Stay calm. You will know everything."

We then began to walk toward the light. The other two figures had disappeared into the light. When we got close to the light, there was a tremendous noise. My head felt like it was exploding. My eyes were burning, and my mouth was dry. I suddenly couldn't remember where we were. It was like I passed out completely.

When I regained consciousness everything was different. I was in this ... thing. I don't know exactly what it was. I could have been in a spaceship, a room, or anything. Everything was tranquil. The lighting was beautiful, and the setting was serene. It looked like a place for relaxing. My head was not hurting anymore and my eyes were fresh, yet I still didn't know where I was. This chamber was unlike any other room I had seen before. It was definitely beyond my imagination and experience. I felt as though I were sitting, although the bench on which I sat was very different from anything I had experienced before.

A figure came to me seemingly out of nowhere. I asked him whether he spoke Italian.

"Yes," replied the figure. "I do speak Italian."

"I would like to know where we are."

Again came the same answer: "In a little while you shall know."

He took me from that room, and we went out. As he had said, everything became clear. I saw everything. I learned everything. The truth of these Strangers was revealed to me!

Once I had absorbed everything, it was time for me to go, but not before we finished our conversation.

The Stranger explained, "Now that you have learned

the truth about who we are, you will return home. When you get home, the first thing you will want to do is get together a parliament of government and tell them that everything you saw and learned is the truth. Tell them everything they think they know about UF0s and aliens is wrong. You need to explain to them clearly what you saw and learned here. You have become the proof of this truth."

"But without physical proof, people will not believe me."

"You will have physical proof for all of them," the Stranger continued. "With this proof, you will not have any problems. Come with me, please."

Then the three Strangers took me to a different place, beautiful and calm. When we got there the Stranger said, "With this Gianni, we are finished. We have demonstrated everything that is important for you to know. Please be comfortable and relax. In a few moments you will return home."

I thanked him, relieved that I would soon be reunited with my family.

Returning To the Present

My eyes became heavy. They were starting to shut by themselves, but when I woke up I found myself in the same place I was before. I looked around and stood up, but I didn't see anything but darkness. It seemed like time was standing still. According to my watch, only ten or fifteen minutes had passed. It all felt like a dream. I looked around again, and I saw my working bag. Near the bag was something round, like a ball, with a metallic chrome finish. It was very light. I put the ball in my bag and started for home.

As I walked toward my house, I was calm and relaxed. I felt happy. I felt very light on my feet. I felt that something had happened. Arriving at home, I opened the door and looked at my family. My heart was beating with joy and happiness, just from seeing my precious and loving family, my children, and my wife.

"Ciao, my dearest family," I exclaimed. "Daddy is home."

My son Michele ran to me with joy, "Daddy! Daddy! It is marvelous that you arrived!"

My daughter Nina followed him. "Yes, Daddy, it is a pleasure to see you at home!"

My wife, Anna, walked toward me. She looked at me with a smile and joy on her face and said, "My love, did you have a good day at work? You look a little bit different! Look! Come, come! Let me see you! Your face is much different, much younger looking and fresher! What happened?"

"Please give me a glass of water," I said. "And a little time. Then I will explain everything to you and the children."

"Very well dear," she replied. "Everyone come here and sit. Dinner will be ready shortly."

"O.K., Anna. If dinner is almost ready, it is better for us to sit and finish eating, and then I can explain what happened to me this afternoon, after work."

I noticed Michele looking in my bag. "Dad, what did

you bring me? A ball? What is it?"

"Please, Michele," I said. "Don't touch that. I will explain after dinner."

Half an hour went by. I was still thinking about the situation with the Strangers and the strange world. For me to explain to my family what happened would not be an easy task. I did not want them to think I was crazy.

Anna announced that dinner was ready. "But before we dine," she said, "Daddy will say a prayer."

We bowed our heads and I began. "Father who art in heaven, I pray for forgiveness and health for every situation we encounter. I pray that you bless this food, and I ask blessings upon this family. I pray for help, that I may explain this situation to my family, and to the world. Amen."

After dinner, Anna made a nice espresso, and we drank coffee on the couch in our favorite living area. Our children were waiting with excitement and impatience for me to speak. Although I felt relaxed and calm, the calm was mixed with enthusiasm and tension. I was in this situation because I was happy to talk to my family about this occurrence.

"So, my dear family!" I began. "I hope that you will understand what I am about to tell you, and that you will believe me after I tell you my story. It was about 7:30, when I was ready to come home. I was looking at the farm to see if everything was alright before I departed. I saw everything was good, so I decided to sit down under the fig tree before I walked home. You all know that I like my favorite tree."

Telling the Story

"So, dad, what happened? Michele prodded.

"Michele!" Nina scolded him impatiently. "Listen so that Daddy can tell us what happened"

"Alright, kids, just listen," Anna said, with a firm but gentle look that told me she recognized the importance of the story I was about to tell.

I continued. "It seems I closed my eyes for a moment. What happened next was like a dream. I saw a strong light and began to breathe very rapidly. I opened my eyes and stood up, but I could not do anything. I couldn't walk. I couldn't scream. I felt paralyzed. I decided to try to slow my breathing, hoping I could relax and understand what was going on."

As I paused, Anna asked me if I wanted another espresso. I declined.

Michele was impatient. "So, Daddy, what happened? What was there?"

I went on with the story. "After I saw that bright light, other lights came on. They were very bright and opaque, with an orange or yellow hue. I had never seen this type of light before in my entire life!"

I could tell by looking at my family that they were astonished. They were waiting for me to elaborate on the situation, but were trying to let me tell the story at my own pace.

Finally, Anna softly asked, "My dear, what kind of lights were they?"

"I don't know. All I can say is that they seemed to be from another world."

I listened to my words, hardly believing them myself. But I knew what I had experienced. I forced myself to continue the narrative.

"Then I saw a figure walking toward me. At first, it looked like a strange figure, like a typical alien you would see on television or read about in a book. He had a huge head, long arms and fingers, and a small body. But as he came close to me, he changed."

"What are you saying, Dad?" Nina asked. "What do you mean 'different'?"

I stopped talking for a few moments. I wanted to consider carefully what to say to them next, so they wouldn't be hurt or confused. I decided to take Anna up on her offer of another espresso. It would at least give me some time to decide how to proceed.

Once Anna brought me my drink, I resumed my narrative. I knew I looked quite intense to them, but I also wanted to convey happiness. Without fear, I continued with the story.

"The figure I saw was different. When it came close to me, it was so tall, much taller than me."

"Taller than you?" Michele asked with surprise.

"Yes, my son, much taller than me. And much bigger than me, too. I believe he was at least two meters tall, probably more. Then two other figures came toward me. When I saw the other two figures, I noticed they seemed to be communicating without talking to each other. And, to my surprise, they were floating in the air."

"Do you mean they had jets on their feet, so they could float?"

"I will explain in a few moments, Michele. I also want to tell you they had no clothes on. They appeared to be naked. I would say they were covered with a metallic skin, light blue in color. I looked at their faces and noticed they had no mouths, noses, or ears. For eyes, what I saw was almost like goggles, bluish-green colors moving back and forth, like the Northern Lights. Depending on what they were saying, the color would change."

The explanation continued for a few more moments, and then Anna got up and said, "Children, it is time to go to bed now. Daddy will continue tomorrow."

The children immediately peppered me with questions, not wanting to wait until the morning to find out about the Strangers. Nina seemed most anxious and asked, "Daddy, the people that you saw, were they good or bad?"

"The Strangers were good," I reassured her.

Chapter Three

The kids kissed and embraced Anna and me, and said goodnight to both of us. After they were in bed, I turned to my wife.

"I don't know what to do with this situation. What I tried to tell you and the kids tonight is much more complicated to explain and it will be hard to hear. But what I am telling you is the truth. It is very different than what we have read in books and what we have seen on TV." I paused. Suddenly I realized how tired I was from the day's events. I asked Anna to be patient with me. "I need to rest before I can finish telling the story to you and the children."

I hugged and kissed my wife. We got ready for bed without saying anything more. When we shut off the lights, I lay in bed with my eyes open for a long time. I could not stop thinking of what happened to me today. Just a few hours ago it felt like a dream, but this was a dream in reality. I was real happy for what I saw and what I participated in. I am to be the proof for our era! Finally my eyes closed and I fell asleep.

I awoke around five in the morning, got up, and made some coffee. I was prepared to go to work. At breakfast I could tell my family was dying to hear more of the story, but even Michele refrained from asking questions. I kissed Anna and the kids, and headed to work.

When I arrived at work, I could not concentrate. My head was throbbing from the experience of the night before. I was trying to decide how to go about dealing with this situation. How can I explain to the world about this great happening? Where should I begin? To whom should I talk? A priest? A lawyer? The president? I was confused, but I needed to do something quickly, the sooner the better.

The day dragged by very slowly. I needed to go home, and tell the rest of the story to my family. This time I would need to show them some proof, so they would believe me and would not think the whole thing was science fiction or some type of illusion. The end of the work day finally came, and I hurried home to my family. When we were together again, I picked up my story where I stopped the night before.

The Ball

"Michele, my son, can you please come over here and bring that chrome ball?"

Nina and Anna were seated on the sofa, while I sat in my usual chair. Michele crossed to my bag to retrieve the ball. He seemed to struggle with it. "Daddy! I have a problem with this ball. I can't move it or pick it up."

I got up and went to see with my own eyes. My son was having a hard time picking up the ball. I called Nina and Anna, and asked both of them to try to pick it up. They both tried to move the ball but could not. Finally, I put my hands on the ball, and it moved. The ball followed me like it had its own energy source. We returned to the living room area, and the ball trailed behind me. As I sat, the ball stopped in mid air, floating. It looked like it was waiting for a sign or a command.

Before I could resume my story, the ball moved from one corner of the house to another. Then with great velocity, it rushed toward me, stopping just in front of my face. I felt like it needed to be touched by me. I placed the palm of my hand on the ball. My hand seemed to activate some kind of energy, and the ball began to pulse with a bright light. The light was intense, almost appearing to send out laser beams. It looked like something was trying to cut through the ball from the inside out. The house was so illuminated that it felt as though the sun was inside our house.

For a moment, Anna and the children remained paralyzed. They didn't know what was going on. Finally, the ball stopped moving, though the light remained. In a flash it simulated all that I had seen with the three Strangers. When Anna and the children saw it, this almost invisible city looked like something out of science fiction or the movies, but this was neither imagination nor illusion; this was real.

It was time for me to tell my family what I saw. But what my family saw was some kind of living quarters in a tall design, something different than our architecture, utterly unlike anything in our style. These living quarters were round. Everything was round, like giant spheres. They were huge. The material used in their construction was different than any we know. No cement, plastic or even wood. The spheres looked like small planets, floating in the air. In places, there were a multitude of spheres, one on top of the other, with a tubular pillar that seemed designed to sustain the rest of the construction. Some elements had two such pillars, some had three, and some had none.

On the ground, we saw beautiful tall mountains everywhere. My family saw rivers, the ocean, trees, flowers. Everything was beautiful. Birds of every kind and color dotted the landscape, along with all kinds of animals living together in a peaceful, controlled kind of way. The sky was beautiful and clear, with no clouds. The sun was calm and warm, not too hot.

After giving my family time to absorb the scene, it was time for me to give them a little more explanation about the situation. "What do you think about all this?" I began.

"It is really strange and extraordinary," Anna said in amazement. "What planet is this? It looks tranquil and peaceful."

"It is very peaceful," I said quietly.

"Dad," Michele said softly, "do they have wars? Or bad people?"

"No."

"There is no war or bad people," Michele said in a dream-like voice. "It is a place with peace and happiness."

"So Daddy," Nina said, "what we see here is almost like imagination, like the movies?"

"This is nothing, my dear. When I tell you what I saw, even more than what you have witnessed today ... it is incredible."

"Tell us what you saw," Michele said.

The Story Continued

With a slight pause, I continued. "I found myself in a room with the Stranger. The walls almost seemed to be made of water. They looked like a mirrors, but very clear. The figure that was with me instructed me to touch the wall. When I did, it opened up like a curtain. Looking out, I saw the sky was really clear. I saw the construction, and the living quarters that looked like spheres or small planets. They were so beautiful to look at. Some were connected to others. The Strangers were everywhere. They were happy and relaxed. I could see no problems. Everyone and everything was tranquil."

Michele interrupted, "What were they doing, all those Strangers?"

"They were doing nothing, just floating and communicating telepathically."

"They were not communicating with any speech or signs?" Nina asked with amazement.

"No, Nina. Like I said, their way of communication is by mental telepathy. There was no other type of communication, no telephones. Life there is much different than our lives here."

"So what kind of life is there?" Nina continued. "Seems to me there is nothing to do there. With a world like this, that looks like ours, with the sun, the moon, the trees, and everything we have here on earth, it still seems so different."

"Yes, my dear, the world there is very different."

No one spoke for a moment. Finally, Anna said, "Really, it seems so strange!"

"Yes, my dear," I replied. "It is complicated. I was waiting to see what they would do with me. Then one of the Strangers came to me and said, 'With me please.' They took me by the hand and directed me into another room."

"Why, Daddy?" Michele asked.

"For a moment, I didn't know what they would do to me. Then we entered the room. Everything in the room was different than our home."

"What are you saying?" asked Anna. "How different?"

"It's like Daddy said, Mom," Nina said. "Their buildings aren't like wood, iron, or any other material that we have here on earth."

I took a moment to try to decide how to explain what type of material it was. "The material there is really different than ours. It is a liquid material. You can go through the walls without worrying about opening or closing doors or windows, because this material is controlled by the mind. It seems to me to be the same material they use for the suits that they wear. Everything is connected with the same material, and the material itself is alive. Just by thinking, the material will do as you wish. I recognized this as we entered the room with the three figures. In a split second, I was transformed. I was just like them, with the same type of skin, the metallic chrome suit. My clothes disappeared. We went through the walls and doors like before, but this time it was somewhat different. I felt like I was in control. I could control this liquid material in any way I wanted."

Anna and the children looked at me with surprised faces. They looked stunned.

I continued. "It seemed like we were just floating in the air. Then I turned my head to see where we were, and we were ten to fifteen meters from the point where that we started."

"So you were walking—or moving—with no support under your feet?" my wife asked.

"Daddy," Nina said, "it seems like a dream, or something you would see in a movie."

"Yes, yes," Michele added, "just like in the movies, Daddy!"

"Yes, my dears. For a moment I thought it was a dream also. Then I looked down and saw the ground. I felt like I was a thousand meters in the air, just floating. It was so beautiful, almost impossible to believe. We moved from one spot to another, like flying without being afraid. Like I said, it felt like a dream. We were moving from one place to another and looking at everything around us."

Clones

I continued my story. "I turned my head, and I saw the three figures. I was astonished when I saw their faces. I asked them, 'Are you triplets? Pardon me, I want to ask you again, are you triplets?' One of them replied in a gentle way, and said, 'No, my friend. We are not triplets. We are clones.' The first Stranger continued. 'This situation is a little complicated to understand, but in a little time it will all make sense. You will see everything clearly.'"

"A few minutes went by. I looked back and discovered we were quite some distance from where we started. Then, in an instant, we were right back on the ground. All of a sudden my feet touched the terrain. The Stranger exclaimed, 'Do you know what this is? Do you know where you are?' 'Yes,' I replied. 'It seems to me that this is earth, with all beautiful plants and trees.' 'Very well,' the Stranger said, 'this looks familiar to you.' 'Why wouldn't it?' I asked. 'It feels like the planet earth, with trees and vegetation. Everything is so green and so healthy. But I don't understand what you are trying to tell me! Is this planet earth? Please tell me if it is.' The Stranger paused for a moment. 'We would like to show you a little bit more, and then I believe you will learn what we are trying to tell you.'"

"We moved on, and in a split second we were in a different area. We were moving like the wind, climbing higher than the trees, then soaring above the mountains. Everything was so green and colorful, like I had never seen in my lifetime. The Stranger looked at me. 'You are very excited Gianni, but you seem tranquil and not nervous.' I thanked him, and in fact I was very relaxed. But I was also astonished and surprised. 'Tell me why,' the Stranger said. 'Because what I am seeing here today is not what I remember reading and watching on television about other worlds. You know what I am trying to say, right?' 'Yes,' said the Stranger, 'we know what you are trying to say, and we do understand.'"

"We continued on our journey, passing by the mountains. It was so beautiful, joyful, and peaceful that I had peace of mind. Above us there were birds everywhere. For a moment I felt that the Strangers were communicating with all the birds. We were in the air with the birds, somewhere between one thousand and fifteen hundred meters in height. I felt so light, like a cloud. Then the Stranger put his hand on my shoulder."

Chapter Four

"Gianni! Gianni! Look, what do you see?"

He called me by my name! This was the first time. "How do you know my name is 'Gianni'? I never told you, right?"

"Yes," the Stranger said. "You are right. We have the power to read your mind. It is what you would call telepathy."

"How do you know how to read minds? How do you learn that? It is a tremendous power."

"When we finished going around the world," the Stranger replied, "everything will be explained to you."

Then I saw a something that was impossible to believe. A place as brilliant as a mirror, with shades of green and blue. It was the ocean. It was so peaceful, calm, clean. In one moment we were above the ocean, floating without touching the water. I bent over and I touched the water with my hand. It was fresh and cold. We remained there for a little while, just looking at the ocean, observing how brilliant and beautiful it was. I saw birds of all different colors and species flying around me. You can't imagine.

After a while, the Stranger again touched my shoulder and said—or rather, communicated telepathically—that we were going to the bottom of the ocean.

"How is it possible to go there without any breathing apparatus?" I asked. "How will we breathe?"

"Don't worry about it," he reassured me. "As soon as you touch the water, the suit that you have will protect you."

As we descended into the water, the metallic blue suit that I was wearing immediately covered my head, like an extra layer of skin. I found I was able to breathe normally. I could see everything clearly, even under water. The three Strangers all looked the same. The way I was moving underwater was the same as I would be moving in the air. Traveling through the ocean, I saw beautiful fish, both small and large. All seemed friendly, and I found I was not afraid of any of them. We went down deep—I would estimate about one thousand meters—so deep that it seemed to me to be an abyss in the ocean. My body was regular, without any pressure or loss of breath. My body was functioning normally, without any complications.

At this point in my story Anna got up and asked if I would like a cup of coffee or tea? I told her I would like some tea. Nina took the pause as an occasion to voice her impression: "Daddy, the way you are telling the story, it sounds like it is heaven, with angels. They all look alike."

"The tea is ready," Anna called from the kitchen. "Would you like it now or after dinner?"

"If it is ready, I would like to have it now," I replied.

She brought me the tea. I began to drink it, but in my mind I was thinking about nothing but the world I had seen. Anna came and sat next to me and told me that in a couple more minutes dinner would be ready. In the meantime I continued telling my story.

After we emerged from the ocean, we traveled toward the greenest forest I had ever seen. There were large valleys of green between the mountains. When we arrived in a certain area, we stopped. We were about sixty centimeters above the ground. I touched the grass. It was beautiful and soft, and it smelled fresh and healthy. I saw flowers the color of yellow and white, like cotton. Beautiful colors, all colors, red, green, orange. All types of plants surrounded by all types of butterflies by the millions, just flying around. The view was overwhelming, and I was elated with happiness.

The Green Planet

By now it was time to have dinner. So my family and I got up and went to the dining room area to eat. When we finished dinner, I got up and went outside, just to look at the sky. Seeing the stars made me happy. The only thing in my mind was the time I had spent in the other world. After several minutes, I went back inside. Everyone was done with dinner.

Michele was waiting to for me, eager to hear the rest of the story. I told him I could relate a bit more, but then we would need to go to bed. He and Nina agreed. We returned to the living room and made ourselves comfortable. It was about seven thirty in the evening. Anna observed that the ball was still in the same position. It had not moved since the previous night. The only change was that it was no longer clear. It was dark. I told her it was

29

waiting for my command. I resumed my story, picking up where I had left off before dinner.

"After I saw all those beautiful creatures, along with the plants and flowers and trees, we began to rise above the trees. We went through the trees, and like I said, everything was beautiful and green. The air smelled like perfume. Everything was glorious. Then we flew high above the trees, accelerating rapidly. Suddenly, I saw myself above an enormous lake. The lake was crystal clear, as blue as the sky, clean and pristine, with all kinds of animals around the lake. Everything was very peaceful. I was just floating around with these Strangers. They were showing me what kind of planet this was. We went through the forest, and it was great. We were floating effortlessly through space and time. It is just hard to imagine how extraordinary this was. It was a tremendous experience. It was like paradise, a heavenly place. I saw all kinds of creatures, from reptiles to lions, sheep, cattle, horses, and tigers. Some of the beasts were new to me; I had never seen them before, and could not imagine what they were. Everywhere I looked, there was no violence, no aggression. Everything was peaceful. The vegetation was magnificent. It felt like the temperature was perfect. It was a fantastic world."

After all this, I had a question for the Strangers. "What is the temperature of this world?"

"Dear Gianni," he replied, "the temperature here is normal. We have the same temperature every single day."

"Really?" I asked incredulously. "It never changes?"

We continued to float toward the mountains. I was

curious to see what I would find out there in the mountains. When we ascended to the top of the mountains, I saw something else extraordinary. Everything was green, all the rivers and lakes were crystal clear. Waterfalls were everywhere. We stood there just for a few minutes, high up in the sky. Then we flew toward one of the waterfalls. One of the Strangers told me to get close to the waterfall, to touch it with my hands. They wanted me to drink it. I did what the Stranger said and drank the water. It was fantastic, so delicious. The sense of the air and the taste of the water was the same. The air was refreshing, and everything was clean.

Then the four of us floated up to about fifteen hundred meters in the air. When we stopped, I saw a beautiful big city. We were high enough to see the enormousness of this city. What I saw were buildings, but not buildings like we are used to seeing. I saw people floating like the three of us were, and they were happy and full of joy. I saw no animosity, nothing but joy. I saw many of them salute each other, but not like we salute each other. They did not exchange words. The only thing they did was make an X across their chests with their arms. Even without them speaking, I understood what was going on. I looked at the Strangers, and I was able to understand this different way of communication. Then I saw other Strangers coming close to me by the thousands. Each was wearing the same suit we were wearing.

Chapter Five

Some had different colors, but the suit was the same. As we went by this beautiful city, everything was brilliant, like chrome. We floated above the city, and slowly we began to descend to the ground. It was tranquil and beautiful, and the ground was green. Then suddenly we were floating over this terrain. The terrain was also covered with the same material as our suits. Everything was brilliant, looking like nothing I had ever seen before in my life. They had no machines, ships, or anything but themselves. There were no motors, no smog, or anything unnatural.

As we moved from one area to another, I asked, "Why do you not have any machines or any means of transportation?" The Stranger only repeated his statement that he would explain everything to me as soon as we finished our tour of the world.

Those buildings had no windows or doors. I could see no stairs or elevators. But it suddenly dawned on me why they don't need any form of transportation. They can just float wherever they want to go. Little by little, things were becoming clear to me.

I paused my story. It was getting late, and the children had to go to bed. In addition, I was trying to figure out how to explain the rest of the story to the children.

The children pleaded with me. "When are you going to finish the story? How much longer?" Michele said. "Why don't you finish it tonight, Dad?" Nina begged.

"It is long story," I said, "and I have to think about what I should not say, so you will believe what I am telling you."

So the children went to bed. Anna came close to me and gently asked if I would like another cup of tea. I said, "Yes, please." She brought the tea pot and refilled my cup. Then she sat next to me. We watched the ball for a few minutes, although it still hung motionless.

Finally, she turned to me and asked, "Gianni, naturally everything you say is true. This ball is proof of that. The world will be surprised by your story, but what do you think will happen?"

"I don't know," I replied. "This situation is critical. When I finish with the story, you and the children will tell me whether it is possible to believe in a world like the one I describe. I don't know if the world will take this seriously or just mock me. The only proof I have is this ball."

After that we went to bed. The next morning I got up and was getting ready to go to work. Before I put my jacket on, I caught myself observing the ball for a few minutes. For some reason, I took the ball and brought it to our bedroom, setting it in the armoire.

In the afternoon when I came home from work, we all got together for supper. When we were finished, we gathered in the living room again. I began to tell the rest of the story, picking up where I had stopped the night before.

I wanted to bring the ball back into the living room, so I went to the bedroom to pick it up. But without my touching it, the ball moved. It floated in front of me, and together we went into the living room where the family was waiting. Without any hesitation Michele questioned me.

"Daddy, why does the ball follow only you? It looks like it is alive."

"It is because this ball is my proof. Tonight we are going to see some things, and I will tell you other things with regards to that world."

I paused for a moment and then resumed my narrative.

"We floated from one area to another. I saw everything that I needed to see. After the tour, the Stranger communicated with me telepathically that it was time to go back. The Strangers told me, all three at the same time, that we were going to go up. They pointed toward the heavens, and we went up high into the atmosphere of the planet. From that vantage point, I saw city after city, all looking exactly the same. Everything was shiny, just like heaven. Then we went back down and entered this enormous room. I was not sure what it was. I remembered to ask the Strangers exactly what time it was. It seemed like I was there for a long time. One of them sent me a telepathic message that time was not important there, and that they don't calculate time. I felt really relaxed and comfortable there, like I was really a part of that world. In that big room like a large sphere I tried to be comfortable, and we sat in seats that were made of the same material as our suits and the building materials. This liquid material would form itself however I wanted.

After a while, seven more Strangers entered the room. They all said, "Hello, Gianni. How are you?" I started to stand up, but they told me to please stay comfortable and that they would all sit next to me. As they began to sit, material rose up out of the floor to form seats for them. We were arranged in a large circle, of which I was a part.

After they were seated, something began to take the form of a ball in the middle of the circle. It grew to a height of about ten meters. It had a clear light blue and violet coloring to it. The ball began to emit a small, roaring sound, like thunder. Then I saw something in the ball, something almost impossible to understand. What I saw was the story of the human race from beginning to end!"

I stopped talking and paused a moment to take several deep breaths, before shouting, "The world is damned!"

"Please, my dear," Anna said to me with a look of concern. "What is it? You seem distressed. Please tell us what you saw."

The End of the World

I took another breath before continuing. "I saw the end of the world, so horrifying and ugly that for a moment I didn't want to believe what I saw when the ball turned dark.

After that, one of the Strangers said me, "Gianni, everything that you learn here, you have to understand, is part of your world. All you saw will occur sometime in the twenty-first century of your time. The old human race will get destroyed. Not even one will survive. All the destruction will occur in your world in three days. The human race will become diseased and crazy, day after day. Everything will be out of control. Humans will kill one another and will destroy everything that lives. But what we want to show you is the beginning of the human race in the world. I hope you will understand what we are trying to do."

Within the ball, things changed rapidly. All the colors were changing. The ball was making new pictures. I looked at the ball and saw a new world. It was beautiful. It looked like their world, without buildings, machines, or anything I was used to seeing. Everything beautiful.

Then I saw two people, walking hand in hand. The terrain around them looked like a beautiful garden, and the two people seemed to be nude. But then darkness came upon this ball, and the garden disappeared from my sight. The image of the two people was replaced by a big storm. It looked like it was heavy rain, with thunder and lightning. I saw a world that was not so pretty to live in. I saw villages and people everywhere. It was no longer paradise. They were fighting, screaming, and killing one another. They had bats and spears, and big battles were going on at this time. Then I saw many bodies just lying dead on the ground. Thousands upon thousands of corpses. There were wounded people and blood everywhere. Then the ball turned from dark to clear. I saw new buildings, the shape of pyramids of different types on the four corners of the world. The people were numerous, and there appeared to be several armies. It resembled the Middle Ages. I saw kings and queens with their fancy garments. Suddenly, I saw a city that I recognized, followed by others that were familiar to me. Picture after picture, I saw Rome, Paris, England, America, China, India, and Africa. Again the ball was showing me that the world was changing. The weather had become fierce. Hurricanes and other destructive storms were accompanied by earthquakes and other natural disasters. After all that the ball just illuminated. Then I saw the world nice and blue. No other color, just blue. It looked like a ball of water. Then I saw birds everywhere. Then a peak of a mountain, then trees again. It looked to me that the ocean was receding and the mountains were taking shape again.

For me it was hard to understand what was occurring. I was looking at this ball, and it seemed to me to be the earth. But I was confused because I was looking at the past. I felt dizzy, and I didn't know what was going on. I looked at the Stranger, who said, "Gianni, I know that you feel bad about all of this, but it is the truth. And with what you just saw, I hope you will be aware. You have knowledge of what happened here today. When we take you back home, you need to talk with governments, and make them understand that all this will occur if they don't have an accord. Humans must change their system of living. Otherwise the earth will burn. That's why we brought you here. We know that you are a person with character, valor, and honesty."

Dinner with the Strangers

The Stranger continued. "Now we will relax. We will have something to eat and drink, and then we will show you the past."

"Eat and drink?" I asked. "What do you eat and drink here?"

"You will see and taste, and you will understand how we live here."

We ate all that was prepared. It was served at a large, beautiful dinner table, made of the same crystal material as everything else. In fact, it seemed like the ball became the table, and all the food and beverages as well. I saw what looked like a dish. Near the dish was a glass that looked like a chalice of crystal. But I didn't see anyone to serve us or even to prepare the food. What I saw on those dishes were fruits and vegetables. In the chalice was crystal clear water. Everything smelled great and looked even better.

None of this made sense to me. "Can you please explain to me what's going on here? What is happening?"

"Yes, Gianni," the Stranger replied. "What you are seeing here is the future. Here we eat fruits and vegetables, and we only drink water. The reason is that everything is pure, and we enjoy what nature does for us. And it maintains us. We don't kill to eat or for sport. This is what we do here in our world, the future. We respect our world."

"Who prepares the food?" I asked. "And who brings it to us?"

The Stranger's reply astounded me. "Everything is prepared by itself. It is controlled by us, with the energy around us and nature. Nobody is enslaved by anyone. We are all equal. Let's eat and relax a bit so we can finish the story of the human race for your peace of mind. Alright?"

"Yes, thank you. You are so nice and gentle. I would like to understand this too!"

Right after we finished eating, everything disappeared into nothing. The table changed right in front of my eyes, reverting to the ball again. Before I could blink, the ball resumed its presentation. Again the ball became bright and dark, and bright again. It became like the planet earth. I felt like I was flying over the earth. I saw the earth and all its beautiful colors, the water, the clouds. From far away I saw people walking. The scene enlarged so that I was able to see eight people walking, covered with clothes. On their heads they wore linen cloth. Then I saw animals of all kinds walking all over the place. Then the ball became dark, and then bright. It showed me battle after battle. I saw many dead bodies. Then the ball changed color again, and I saw three pyramids. I saw kings. I saw people battling. And I saw thousands of slaves. Dead bodies were everywhere. The ball changed color again, and I saw a great city. I recognized it immediately. It was Rome. But it was so beautiful and clean. I saw thousands of Roman soldiers. I saw the soldiers everywhere around the world, and no matter where they were, I saw dead people. After that the ball became black. It looked like a marble. Then it became gray, and it showed me thousands upon thousands of people dead.

War / Death

Then I saw airplanes, tanks, armored cars. Bombs were exploding all around. People were fighting against people everywhere—in the air, on the land, on the ocean.

It looked as though it was the Second World War. Then the ball changed to red, dark red.

Chapter Six

Then the ball changed back to gray. I saw that Europe was destroyed. Thousands of people dead, buildings down, bridges blown apart from England to Russia. Then the ball changed color again, becoming crystal clear.

Before finishing the story, I stopped and looked at my family and said, "My dear family, the story is almost over." They looked at me, transfixed. I could see the fear in their eyes.

Then the ball changed color. It was hard to tell if it was green or blue. Something was happening in the future, and again I had difficulty understanding what was happening to our planet. This time I saw people who were sick by the millions. Some were dying because of the wars, but many others were dying from disease and famine. I saw civilizations and countries destroyed. The destruction was so wide spread that it was hard to believe what was happening. Then the ball showed me hospital buildings full of people, all sick and dying every day.

I was sad, very sad. I said, "This is impossible. That will not happen to my planet!"

Then the Stranger gently put his hand on my shoulder and said, "Dear Gianni, what you see is happening now. The reason you don't know is because governments don't tell you the truth. But what you are going to see … your future will be ugly. It will be painful for you, your family, and the whole human race."

Then I saw a glass coming toward me. It had water in it, and the Stranger told me to drink it so that I could be relaxed.

The ball changed color, and I saw again the planet earth. After that the ball showed me again what was going on, and I saw a lot of confusion all over the world. In every part of the world, in country after country, the governments were agitated and out of control. It was some kind of desperation. Then the ball changed in color, becoming blood red before it became bright again. It looked to me like the whole world was at war. The worst thing I saw was something very, very different, but instantly recognizable: nuclear missiles flying from one country to another. I saw a nuclear warhead make impact, and there was a huge explosion followed by a catastrophic ball of fire over Asia. It was similar to the tell-tale mushroom clouds from the bombings of Hiroshima and Nagasaki, but ten times more destructive.

Then the ball changed color again to black, and then to red again as before. The ball showed me something new. I hoped what I was seeing was not what I thought it was, but my hope was in vain. What I saw was the end of the world. The demonstration showed me the planet earth burned and scorched, not just in sections, but the whole planet, burning like the sun. The ball showed me the earth, moon, and sun from a distance. From far away, they looked like three suns.

Having finished that section of my story, I rested my eyes for a few seconds. My eyes were sore, and I started to cry. With a deep breath, I managed to say to my family, "My dear family, what I saw and what I am telling you will indeed happen in our time. The human race is going to self-destruct. For now, my duty is to speak with the governments of the world, even though I know they will think I am crazy. But now I don't know what to do or where to go."

It was getting late, and we were all tired, so we decided to go to bed to get a good night of rest. The next morning Anna and I awoke in the early morning. We had a cup of cappuccino, and slowly the day came to life. The kids were getting ready to go to school. We kissed them, and they were on their way. An hour went by, and Anna said she needed to go to the market. I gave her a hug and a kiss, and I said goodbye to her. I was now by myself at home. I had decided not to go to work today. I needed to stay home and reflect on everything I had seen and what I needed to do. I knew I would have to be very careful about what I said and to whom I said it. For a time I was worried for my family, because I wasn't sure if they believed what I was telling them or not. Even though I had seen these things, it was even hard for me to believe. And then here I am trying to go out in the world to talk to the leaders of the nations and to get them to believe me without them thinking this is just another UFO story. But even if they do believe me and they do take my message seriously, then I have to worry about what the leaders of the world will do to me and my family.

The day went by fast. Anna returned from the market, and our children returned from school. Anna prepared something to eat, and after we ate I continued with the story.

After I saw the three suns burning, the ball changed from color to pure black, like the night. Then right before my eyes it became crystal clear before suddenly disappearing. The Stranger told me everything would be explained after the destruction of the world.

"Gianni," the Stranger began, "stay calm and relax. The next scene that you will see is your future and our past. It will be very difficult to understand, but we will explain it to you in a very easy and comfortable way."

His voice was calm and relaxed, without any worries. He went on. "Before the end of the world, your country Italy, along with Britain, France and Germany, had control of the world order. Fifteen years before World War Four, they had all the nuclear power in the world, as well as chemical weapons. They came together and decided they would make a world of perfect humanity. They assembled the world's top scientists in genetic engineering, who worked night and day until they found what they believed was a formula to create this perfect human being. In doing so, they were trying to develop an army of these humans to protect the earth in a way that had never occurred before. So they developed and then built a spaceship the size of a soccer field. They put in it the most advanced scientists, doctors, engineers, and mathematicians. The crew consisted of the best pilots in the world. The spaceship was designed with a self-sustaining nuclear power source. They had the capability to orbit the earth for many years. They could develop new ideas. They could develop ways to study atmospheric conditions. They had at their disposal all the best technology and the most intelligent people from among the human race. The people on the spaceship were in excellent health. They were all attractive. And each and every one of them was of white European descent."

Spaceship Lab

"At last, the spaceship took off from planet earth, into outer space. The situation down on the earth continued to deteriorate. So soon after the launch, the Fourth World War began. The scientists in the spaceship received little information about the war, as communication grids were among the early targets in the war. Within a short amount of time, all communication between the spaceship and earth was lost. The scientists were cut off from their home world. Eventually, weak signals from the planet began to be picked up, mostly ground communications sent during the war that were only now catching up with their ship. The details were few, but they were able to piece together enough information to learn that the earth was destroyed. It was impossible for them to return. Life on earth was no longer possible because the earth was burning. At the same time, it would be centuries before they would arrive at another habitable planet.

"Despite the seeming futility of their task, they continued their work. Many years passed, and the creation of the perfect human began. Eventually they were the first of our ancestors. They were created in space. Soon, the ship was inhabited with many of these new creations. Then the clones were created. They were superior to the first creations. They had higher intelligence and better health. Inevitably, the humans slowly died off until only the clones remained.

"The clones took responsibility for the spaceship. Many years went by, during which the clones had time to study. They learned the original purpose of the ship. So they began to develop a different body, a healthier body. The capacity to build and fabricate was very easy for them. They were able to do anything. Their capacity for learning new skills and completing new tasks was almost infinite. After many decades, their advanced minds were able to develop telepathic and telekinetic abilities. In time, the clones grew into a populace of one thousand.

"A new communication skill was born in that spaceship. Everything in life would be precise and pure. They discovered they could manipulate liquid into any material. This allowed them to create many things using their minds. With this, construction of a new spaceship began. In the new spaceship, there was no electricity, fuel, or even nuclear energy to power the ship. Everything was done by the clones' telekinetic powers.

"New living quarters were created in the new spaceship, which was shaped like a ball. These new living quarters were capable of sustaining life while traveling at the speed of light, much faster than the original spaceship. With this capacity, they traveled the universe, planet after planet. They learned how to use the universe's energy and the power of magnetic forces. They studied the gasses and energy in space, learning how to use them for their own gain. Life expectancy for the clones grew to over one thousand years.

"Yes, Gianni," the Stranger said as an aside. "We live for a long time. Death here is almost nonexistent."

"The clones traveled around the galaxy for a while. They knew about earth's existence through records in the ship's computer. They knew Earth's history very well, and with their superior intelligence they could understand everything that had happened to planet Earth. They learned the past and the future. Eventually, they were able to return to Earth's solar system and learn about it firsthand.

"Finally, they came into low orbit around Earth. They saw that everything was peaceful and quiet with no living matter to be seen. They surveyed the planet and saw that everything had been destroyed. There was no vegetation and very low oxygen levels. The oceans were very low and had a dark green color. They found no lakes or rivers, no cities or buildings. Earth was completely burned. They stopped over a large, dry area and landed the spaceship. From the moment they landed, the planet changed.

"Everything that was destroyed disappeared, and new growth came to life. The water was purified, and the world became clean soon after that. Clouds began to appear, and soon after the clouds, rain fell on earth. They did all this by using the remaining ocean water, the energy of the sun, and natural acids from the soil. The rain covered the earth. It rained for many days. When it stopped, vegetation began to grow everywhere. There were all kinds of flowers and trees. Then lakes and rivers began to form. Finally our ancestors developed the world we are in now.

"The clones moved off the spaceship and began to live on earth. They increased to a population of 144,000,000. We are a big family, Gianni. We know each other, we understand each other, and we respect each other, because we are in a new world of a new creation. The world of the past is gone. This is the New World. Ours. The humans of the past can't live here. They have a strong tendency for destruction. They have malice in their hearts. That is why we have you here to learn what is happening to us because of the selfish ways of your people. They want to create better things with no responsibility and no consequences. We will work hard to help you, but we know that will be an unyielding mission for us and for you. We will do our part, but we need you to do your part, so together maybe the old world can be salvaged. Gianni, do you acknowledge all this?"

"Of course," I replied. "I will do what is necessary for the sake of the world and my family."

Chapter Seven

"This is a great story," I said. "The correction of the human race is a birth of perfection. Everything is clear to me now, but still like a dream. But I still have some questions. How did the clones create the fish, birds, and all the other animals? What I saw was all perfect, but its outward appearance was almost identical to animals that I know one earth now."

"Yes, Gianni, I can easily explain to you," the Stranger said. "When the humans went into space, they took numerous samples with them, including all kinds of seeds and eggs, as well as DNA. They had the genetic code for everything the earth could provide at the time. With this material, they were able to study how to make everything better. They changed the quality of the eggs and the seeds they brought with them to genetically correct any flaws. Eventually, our ancestors—the first clones—returned to earth and planted the seeds and developed all living things into perfection. Even the animals had superior intelligence. They also had to change the damaged planet into a perfect world, which they did. All this will last for eternity. All the creatures on earth now have a mental capability for what is good, so they take care of themselves with a high respect for nature. They respect everything around them as we do. Everything on this planet respects all other living things, and everybody and everything is responsible maintaining order. That is why we can say this planet is designed for eternity. No one here hurts anything or destroys anything. We don't need money to support our needs, and we don't need machines or factories to make things to survive. Our health is one hundred percent. Here no one gets sick or hurt, and when it is time to have babies, even that is without pain, because we have a different system. We use our mental capability without limits."

After saying all that, the Stranger looked in my eyes with his green-blue eyes. After a moment, he very calmly asked, "Gianni, what are you thinking? Do you like what I am telling you? I know it is hard to understand, but everything that you have seen is real. I know you believe it is true because I feel the palpitation of your heart and I feel that you are happy with what you have seen. But at the same time you are sad at what you have seen of your past."

"Yes," I admitted, "everything I saw of the past has made me sad, but if the world is going to be like that, what can I do? What I've seen here, this makes me happy, because I see a better world. I feel that the world will be a better planet under your control. And if the old world has to be destroyed and all this will happen, what can we do to change the human race?"

"We can't change the history of the world," the Stranger said, "but we need to do our duty. We need to send a message to the earth's population to let them know where humanity is headed. Our hope is that some government will listen to you. With the help of our future, we know we can change the world to be a better place, without changing the past. This is very important to us, because your present is our past. And you, Gianni, you are one of our ancestors! I will explain this to you because you and your children are part of us.

"When your children are about twenty nine or thirty years old, they will be part of a scientific experiment. They will volunteer their DNA. Your daughter will donate some of her eggs, and your son will donate some of his sperm. These will be frozen and will later be part of the experiments to change humanity and to develop the clones. Your daughter will become a doctor, and your son will become a scientist."

"Is that why you chose me and brought me here?" I asked.

"That is one reason. The other is because you are an honest man. You are very intelligent, and you listen when others speak. You have no fear of the unknown."

"I would like to know how you clean the planet. The planet is so beautiful and clean. I have not seen any trash. Where do you put all the unhealthy material like debris and rotten material?"

"We don't need to clean anything," he explained. "The system that we have here cleans itself. The things that are no longer good disintegrate and get consumed by the ground. They are pulverized and become part of the earth again. Because we consume only fruits, vegetables, and natural things, and only drink water, everything is natural. Nature will accept and consume everything, and all things become clean."

I was fascinated by the implications of all this. "Then there is no problem with trash or any type of pollution."

"No problem at all," the Stranger replied.

Now that I had a chance to ask questions, my curiosity began to overflow. "Can you tell me how you accomplish time travel?"

Speed of Light

The Stranger explained. "This material we use is like a second skin. It is the same material that the ball and all the buildings that you see are made of. Everything around us is made from this material. We call it natural liquid skin. With our mental capabilities, we think of what we need and this material will form according to our need. It will stays in our body like a protective shield. We can travel anywhere we want from place to place. The only thing we need to do is think and we will go there. Our desire is like a command to this material."

I looked at the skin that I had on, and I looked around and thought, "Everything I see and touch is all liquid. It is unbelievable."

Then I heard the voice of the Stranger in my head. "Yes, Gianni, everything is liquid. As for space travel, when we are ready to travel into the past, we will let you know. We will show you how. But right now I want to take you down so we can show you the museum that we have of past earth."

So we descended and landed, and we found ourselves in another ball. This ball suddenly moved, and we were taken to a very odd looking place that the Stranger called a museum. It looked to me like another ball the size of a small planet.

Inside I saw things of the past. I saw the pyramids, the Coliseum, and castles. I saw big towers and skyscrapers. I saw all types of machines, buses and cars, ships, and factories. I saw countries, one of which was the United States. Then I saw Europe and Africa and all of the continents. What they were showing me was my world, the planet earth, the earth of their past and my present. I learned that everything was registered in this ball, thousands of years of earth's history. The ball showed me things in rapid succession. Everything was three dimensional, and I could see everything clearly. It was similar to what I had seen prior to this, but this time I was getting more information. It was showing me more of the problems of the world.

After watching for a while, I realized I was only seeing things in my past. "Why are you showing me the past and not the future?" I asked the Stranger.

The Strangers each looked at me, and I looked at them. I saw sadness and sorrow in their faces. Finally, the first Stranger spoke.

"Gianni, forgive us if we make you feel bad, but I have to say that the past is also important for us because it is our future. What we are trying to do is to understand our lives so we can understand also what happened in the past. It will enable us to change what was wrong. We were created from humans. Our life here is very different from our lives on the past earth. We are human, but at the same time we are not humans. Our creation began from you in the past. It was completed in the future with perfection, without flaws. We developed a perfect atmosphere and perfect life here. As you have seen, no one here has any diseases, no one suffers, and we don't disturb nature. Everything is perfect here. You know we eat fruits and vegetables, and we only drink water. Everything we do here we do with joy, and it is done for the benefit of all. We can control the future and the past, and with your help we can visit the past with no danger and no risk of damaging our history. We can go through past, present, and future at any time."

"Why me?" I asked again. "There are so many people much more intelligent than I am, more capable of convincing governments and heads of organizations of the past world like you want me to do."

The Strangers explained as we continued to move through the museum. "Very well, Gianni. We want you to know why we chose you out of all those of your twenty-first century. We chose you because you go back thousands of years with a pure bloodline, as do your children. That is one reason for our choice. Another factor is that you are honest, and you come from a profound race, strong in nature. Your race is Calabrese, Romana."

I was surprised at what the Strangers told me, but I was intrigued. Right after this, everything changed inside the ball. The ball showed me the past two thousand years. What I saw was regiments of soldiers in an area that looked like the region of Calabria.

Romans / Calabrians

I saw many soldiers with different uniforms. They didn't look like Romans to me. They had very sophisticated armor, and carried spears, bow and arrows, swords and axes, and fiery weapons. They looked strong and powerful. And they were engaged in battle with the Romans.

Chapter Eight

When the battle between the Romans and Calabrians ended, the Calabrians were victorious. They won over the Romans with a terrible violence. The ball again showed me many years after this battle. The vision that appeared was a castle. In this castle was a duke of high intelligence, a man of deep empathy.

"Gianni," the Stranger said, "the man you see here is part of your family. Those that you saw in the battle are some of your ancestors, and the duke is also your ancestor. We chose you because of your past and because of your genes. So, Gianni, now that you know some of your history, we want to tell you about us and our history. We need to move to another place so we can show you a creation and accomplish what we are going to do. I want you to understand why we are like this. You need to see all with your own eyes."

So after the Strangers and I had the conversation, we all united and we went up in the air from the museum. We were flying through the air into another area of the world. From above I saw a multitude of people, numbering perhaps in the millions. The population was waiting for us. I also saw other Strangers coming from above us and below us, flying all around us. There were men, women, and children everywhere. I became confused and my curiosity led me to wonder why they have children if they are all clones. At first it looked like many races, but in fact it was only one. The place that I was looking at was like a desert, a crystallized desert. It was enormous. There were people flying everywhere, and they were all happy, each wearing the silver chrome suits with their heads exposed. I looked at them and was impressed. They all had the same look: the same light blue eyes, the same jet black hair. They were beautiful. Their facial features were so delicate and perfect. They all had white skin, and they all had a smile on their face.

Then the Stranger said, "Look, Gianni! Whatever you see down below and all around you is the future. This will be accomplished by the human race. This is far, far in the future from where you live. Look to this multitude of people and tell me what you see!"

So I looked for a few moments, and then said, "Before I tell you what I see, I want to ask you a question. You know everything about me, my family, and my world, but what I know about you is what you tell me and what I see. So by seeing this and by hearing you I believe it is all true and honest."

"Naturally, Gianni, if we wanted to deceive you we could have done so right from the beginning. And not just with you but with many others. We could have played games with you and the world. We could also engage in malice and destruction if we wanted to. We could destroy your world any time we wanted. We are much more intelligent than the old human race, but we are also full of love and caring. We love creation and nature. We respect ourselves, and we respect human nature from the past and the future."

"Thank you so much, my friend," I said. "This is a lesson that I will remember forever."

We descended to the ground, and I found myself amidst the population. I felt tranquil and relaxed. I also found that I knew everyone, and at the same time they knew me. It was a very strange feeling. I felt in my mind that all of them said, "Hello, Gianni. It is a pleasure to know you." After this my friends and I went up in the air again. From up above I saw all those people taking off and disappearing into the air. I noticed they were going in different directions. I could see the sky full of them. I followed the three Strangers, and we returned to the sphere where we began our journey.

One Kind

When we were once again seated in the sphere, the Stranger looked at me and said, "Gianni, tell me everything you saw and everything that you understood."

"What I saw is that you all look exactly the same. I didn't see any other race or different skin color like we have in our world. You all have white skin and jet black hair. You all have blue eyes, and you are all the same height. Physically you are all the same."

"Yes, Gianni," the Stranger said. "That is exactly what we want to know. The fact is we don't know why we don't have any others! We don't know why this occurred. We don't have any records, so we don't know what happened to the other races. We don't have any idea how to begin to understand this, and to penetrate into the history of the human race. Why was this erased from our records? We have no trace of any kind, and again we need your help. So we chose you, Gianni, from the past because of what we discovered about you. We did try with many other humans before you. We took some Chinese, some Indians, some Africans, and people from both North and South America. We took some from Europe and from all over the world. But with all these people, we still could not reach any conclusions. We tried and tried again over the centuries. But, finally, we came to a moment of truth. It was you and your family."

"What is it that you are saying?" I asked, uncertain where this was leading. "My family? My children and my spouse?"

"Gianni, my friend, be calm. Don't be afraid. We are trying to tell you about your family because we are part of you, just as you are a part of us. That is why you were chosen for this agenda. So we can finish what we need to finish. After this visit here, Gianni, we will take you back so that you can help us."

"My dear friend," I said, "you are asking me to help you! But I don't know what to do!"

With a smile on his face the Stranger said, "Don't worry about it. We will tell you what to do and what to say. First, you need to tell your family about this. After that, it will be easier for you tell others. You will have some difficulties, and you will have hard times with the people with whom you will speak, because the majority will not believe you; they will think this is another UFO dream or your imagination. It will be hard for you to deal with the situation without our help, and we know this."

With a concerned look, I exclaimed, "My friend, I don't understand! You are telling me that you are going to help me with this? Are you coming with me? And will you speak with me to the governments and high ranking people of the past planet earth? Are you going to demonstrate your physical capability and your telepathic powers, and all the other powers that you have? After that they will believe you and me. They will believe that you can make this world better and organize this for the future!"

After I questioned them, I waited for a response, but what I saw was them looking at each other. It looked to me like they were communicating telepathically, because I couldn't hear any sounds coming from them. After all this, all three of them fixed their eyes on the sphere intensely. I saw the sphere in the center like a liquid, clear as crystal. It developed into a sphere as large as a soccer ball. It was floating in the air.

Finally the three of them looked at me and said, "Gianni, this sphere or ball—whatever you want to call it—is all you need. This will be sufficient proof. You have to understand that we can't come with you because at this point the humans of the past are very confused and complicated."

"I understand that," I said, "but you don't have a problem with me, and I am also a human from the past."

"Your situation is different," they said. "You have an advanced mentality, and you can reason. You know how to listen when someone speaks to you. The majority of human beings don't have the capacity to listen or reason. A conversation to the average person is either the gossip of others or the invention of stories. The few that have the ability to reason and converse are the people on whom we are counting. The human race is dangerous. We can't have any contact with the humans of your time, and if we come with you and disturb the past we also disturb the future. If we do just one thing against the laws of time, we will not exist."

The Messenger

"We have to be very careful how we deal with this; that is why we have you. You are the door for us to get in and reason with everyone. You will be a messenger for us. You will do whatever you can to convince your people. We will follow you from the future with the sphere."

They told me all that and more, whatever was necessary for me to understand the task ahead. Then they continued with the conversation, showing me other things. When they were finished, we came together just as at the beginning. We sat and ate the beautiful vegetables and fruit, along with a nice glass of fresh water. We went out after eating, and we flew into the air again. We were inside this huge ball that I now called a sphere. It was the same shape as it was when I got in the first time in the past. The four of us went up in the air.

As we ascended, the Stranger said to me, "Gianni, look for the last time on this world of the future. I want you to remember all you saw and all you did here. What you see is the truth. The ideas about UFOs and aliens from outer space that your people have are completely false. What they believe is not the truth."

After he told me that, we went up a little higher, up around that beautiful planet that I call New Earth, for the last time. Then I felt that the ball that I was in started to change formation. It started to look different from what I was used to seeing. I saw the Strangers coming toward me. The four of us held hands together, and without words I heard, "Goodbye for now, Gianni, dear friend." Soon after that I saw a bright light, and then all became dark. Whatever happened next I don't know. When I woke up, I found myself at the same place I was when they first approached me. I looked at my watch; it felt like time stopped.

I was confused and light headed. I felt strange. I said to myself, "Is this a dream or for real?" I got ready to go home. I made sure I had everything with me. On my way home, I felt fresh and new. I was not tired. It was getting dark, and the time to get home and have dinner was drawing near. I thought that I wouldn't know how to tell you what just happened to me! But you must believe me! I had to take a chance!

After I parked the car, I sat in the driveway for a while reflecting on how I would begin telling you the whole story without frightening you. One thing that concerned me was that you children would tell your friends. Despite the Stranger's reassurances, my worries were getting bigger and bigger.

Chapter Nine

It came to a point that I had to deal with my family now on a matter of security. I stopped talking for a little bit and looked at my family.

"My dear family," I said, "you know that I love you very much, and I am very happy that I returned home. What makes me happy, though, are the Strangers and that world."

"When everything happened," Anna said, "you said that only fifteen minutes went by. But it seems to me that maybe a week or more went by. I don't understand why."

"Yes, dear," I responded. "Time goes by differently there. And when you travel at the speed of light, you can travel for years and years without change. Years go by, but you stay the same."

After we had the conversation about the situation, we were ready to have dinner. Afterwards we went to bed. The next morning after I woke up, I went straight to the room where the ball was. I felt as though it was calling me telepathically. When I got close to the ball, I put my hand on it. I sensed that I had a message from the ball. A voice in my head said to me, "We are here with you telepathically. We are together. Everything that you need, any help that you are looking for, we are here to help you. You will not be alone."

After I heard that, I began thinking about what I should do first. Where should I go? They told me that I had to speak with competent people who will understand and will have consideration for my story and all the things of which I will inform them. And the only proof I have is the ball. So I decided that I needed to talk to someone in the government, beginning with the Italian government. I had to bring together the most intelligent people, professors of science and medicine, literature, and people involved with architecture and geometry. We would also need doctors engaged in genetic engineering. After I reached that decision, I came to point number one: the government, in particular the Italian government.

I decided I needed to hire one of the best advocates to register and record my message. The day went by quickly just thinking of all these things I needed to do and when I needed to do them. As I sat in the living room mulling over the matter, I noticed Anna standing in the doorway, watching me. I don't know how long she had been standing there, but her presence made me feel comfortable.

"My dear Gianni," she said when she knew I had seen her, "with all this clear information that you have and some that you showed us, do you think someone out there will believe you and take you seriously? Or do you think they will take this as a dangerous situation and become aggravated toward you and your family? Without protection, what will happen to us?"

"Yes, my dear, I know," I assured her. "But I am the only one that can resolve the truth about UFOs and aliens from another planet. Without my sacrifice, the lie will continue forever; people will believe the same bogus thing about aliens and will never know the truth! The Strangers who became my brothers, they need my help. Like I said before my dear, without me they can't accomplish their goals."

"So then, when would you begin with this?" Anna asked.

"Tomorrow, because the sooner the better. I want to be free of this as soon as I can!"

"Tomorrow?" she asked. "Why so soon?"

"I believe we don't have much time!"

"So what do you think you will do tomorrow? Where will you go?"

"My dear, first of all I have to call the lawyer. And then when everything is prepared the next thing I need to do is go to the capital. I also need to write down everything that I saw, the stories that were told to me and everything that happened to me on that future earth with the Strangers, my brothers. Then the lawyer and I will travel to Rome, and with the help of the ball, which I will take with me, I can explain and show them with clarity the truth that was revealed to me."

"Do whatever you need to do, and whatever is best," Anna said with a warm smile. "I will support you. Your family will stand behind you."

"Thank you, honey, for understanding and being united with me in this situation, because I need you and the children to make me feel strong and decisive."

I prepared my typewriter. I started writing, trying to

capture all I had seen and heard, because it was important that I not forget anything, not even a small detail of what happened to me there in that beautiful world. After I finished writing, I called my lawyer, Alberto. We got together, and he advised me on how to make an appointment to see if we could get a date with high ranking government officials.

Then Alberto told me, "Gianni, we are going to take off in a couple of days, but not yet. There is nothing we can do until we hear from the president. As soon as I hear from him, I will call you so that we can get ready and do what we need to do."

"Thank you, Alberto," I said. "We will see each other in a couple of days."

"Goodbye, Gianni," he said, shaking my hand. "And goodbye, Anna. I will see both of you soon."

I told him goodbye, and watched him drive away.

The children, Anna, and I had dinner. We talked for a little while and then went to bed. Then next day I was first to get up. I was excited, nervous, and anxious. I had to prepare myself mentally for what I needed to do. In the meantime the children awoke. They got ready for school and, after giving Anna and me a kiss and a hug, they departed.

"Gianni," Anna asked, "what are you going to do today?"

"First, I am going to go to work and tell my people I am taking a short vacation. Then I will come home and pack my bags to leave."

"When do you think you will leave?"

"Oh, maybe tomorrow or the next day. I need to get started on this matter as soon as possible, because this is very important. It is the best news and information for the world to know."

"You look very nervous, Gianni."

I smiled at her. "No, no. I am not nervous. I am just happy and anxious, and I don't want to lose any time. I can't wait for the moment to arrive so I can speak with the most intelligent people in the world. I just can't wait."

After our conversation, I went to our bedroom. I found myself looking at the ball. Again I put my hand on the ball, and the ball showed me the future. Then the ball changed colors and showed me the face of the Stranger.

The sign that he was giving me was a good sign. I took it to mean that everything would be fine. He was encouraging me and making me feel comfortable and secure. After the vision of his face on the ball, he thanked me for all I was going to do, and he promised to be with me any time I needed him. Then the ball changed to a dark color and that was the end of that. I got up to go to the kitchen where my wife was preparing some sandwiches. I grabbed a cup of coffee and then sat to rest some.

Two days went by before the advocate called me. He informed me that everything was ready to go. We prepared to take off for Rome. I packed everything I needed, including the ball, because it was the best—indeed, the only—proof I had in my hands. The day came to go. I said "goodbye" to my family. We hugged and kissed, and they told me "goodbye."

Depart

We took the train for Lamezia Terme. Once there, we changed to a train called the Arrow, a high speed train, which traveled non-stop from Calabria to Rome. When we arrived in Rome, some special agents from the government were already waiting for us to take us to our destination, the State Palace. Once we got to our room they helped us settle in. Within a very short span of time, one of the agents came to tell us that we were invited to speak with the president, who had assembled the congress and the house.

We escorted to a large ballroom, where I was introduced to all of them. We sat for dinner. After dinner, drinks were served, and then the president approached a podium and called everyone to attention. The strained conversation that had accompanied dinner and drinks immediately came to an end. This was the focal point of the evening they had been told to expect.

"Ladies and gentleman," the president began, "please bear with me for a few moments. I am honored that our country has been chosen to be the recipient of this important message. It is crucial that tonight we listen attentively, because what we are going to hear is of grave importance to our future. I personally was informed of this news a few days ago, and I thought it necessary to convene all those who are present tonight. And now would like to introduce to you Mr. Alberto Masi.

Alberto took his place at the podium. "Thank you very much, Mr. President. I appreciate this welcome. Thank you to the house and to the congress, and thank you to those who prepared this fantastic dinner. I am here to accompany my friend and cousin, Gianni, a man with an extraordinary message. I encourage you to listen to him tonight, because his message is an urgent one. Therefore, at this time I would like to introduce to you my friend and cousin, Mr. Gianni Masi."

I stood up and walked toward the podium, while the gathered members applauded politely. I shook the president's hand, then turned and embraced Alberto. They took their seats as I turned toward the people present. I looked at them, and I saw their faces, each of which had a nervous smile. I lowered my head and then slowly lifted it to look at the ceiling. I took a deep breath and began.

"Thank you very much. Mr. President, members of the government, ladies and gentlemen, I thank you for this opportunity to speak to you. Please excuse me if I am a little nervous, but also proud of what I have to tell you. I have a lot to say, but our time is short. We don't have much time to lose. But I believe that after you hear my story, we will be united more than ever. Tonight I will tell you why I came here to talk to you. What I am going to tell you is just a little part of my story."

Giovanni Rocca

Chapter Ten

The Speech

"Ladies and gentlemen, I am a family man with no power whatsoever, and I work every single day to keep my family alive. I study, and I read the papers and books. I read human-interest stories, and I read scientific articles. I think my intelligence is normal. Like yourselves, I watch television for what is going on the world, and I would assume you know pretty much the same things I do. What I am trying to tell you is that I am nothing special, but tonight what you will hear from me will be special.

I began to tell them the story of what happened to me that night. What I told them was what happened to me that night from the point that they took me to the point of no return. I told them almost everything, just as I had I told my family. After finishing my narrative I paused and said, "Dear friends, I will end with this for tonight. This is just the beginning of the saga. I have a lot more to tell you. I will need another meeting to complete this story. I hope that you take the time to come for the next meeting for the conclusion of this good news. Again, I thank you for this opportunity to speak to you, and I beg you to come again tomorrow night to hear the end of this saga. Thank you very much."

After the speech, I remained at the front for a few minutes. People had questions for me, but I gave them very vague answers. Eventually, I extracted myself from the crowd. I made my way over to the president to ask him a few things about the following night. I asked him to encourage people to come back so I could finish telling them what I had to say.

"Don't worry, Mr. Masi," the president assured me. "You will have everything you need tomorrow and everyone will come. In return, what I want is evidence that will provide proof that what you are saying is true. I don't want to look like a clown and be laughed at. I want everyone to believe and trust not just me but also you."

"Mr. President," I continued, "I would like you to open the doors for these people tomorrow night, so that you will see what will occur. I promise you I will have evidence that will show that everything that I am telling you is the truth. May God help us all because what is coming is not pretty. The future is dangerous and dire. Because you are the head of the country you have a tremendous responsibility to control this information for the sake of the world."

"Very well," the president said gravely. "We will see you tomorrow. Now let us go home and rest, because tomorrow will be a big day. Goodnight."

I said goodnight to him and Alberto, and I returned to my hotel. The night passed, and the next morning we got up and had breakfast. I told Alberto that I needed to go back to my room to make sure that the ball was in my suitcase. When I got to the room, I opened the suitcase. It was empty. I began to panic. The ball was the only proof I had. I began to search the room, but I could find no sign of the ball anywhere. My heart was beating very fast. I was nervous and scared. The future of the planet literally rested on that ball. It took all my effort to calm down. I decided call Anna to see if the ball was at home.

Before I could dial the number, I heard a noise like the wind whistling behind me. Then suddenly something flew in front of me and transformed right before my eyes. It was the liquid material I had seen in the future. The ball became clear like a mirror, and it changed to form the face of the Stranger, my friend. My worries quickly dissipated.

"Hello, Gianni," the Stranger began. "How are you? I hope everything is well there. Remember that we are with you every step of the way. As long as you have the ball, we are with you. Don't worry if at times you don't see the ball, because we control the ball also. Relax and know that we see you at all times."

We said goodbye and I thanked them. Again the ball disappeared in the air. Afterward, I was tranquil, because now I knew that I had real help from them."

Around noon the next day, Alberto entered the room. "Gianni!" he called. "Is everything all right? Are we going to do what we need to do today?"

"Everything is fine!" I assured him. "Just the way it should be."

He suggested that we find somewhere to have lunch, and I agreed. After that we took a walk, but found two agents waiting for us with a limousine. They were waiting to take us to the presidential palace. We had an appointment with everyone at two o'clock. I returned to my room to get ready. I changed clothes and was ready to go. When we arrived at the presidential palace there were a lot of people there. More would soon be coming. They all said hello to me, and I replied with a hello back to them.

We moved into the lobby of the palace. In the presidential palace were all kinds of important people. There were representatives of religions, representatives of the military, representatives of science and medicine and professors. After a while, someone who looked official pushed his way through the crowd. "It is nice to meet you, Mr. Masi," he said. "I am Pietro Gaetano, the secretary of defense. I need a few words with you now, and we shall talk more later, after the meeting.

Secretary Gaetano approached the podium. "Ladies and gentlemen, I would like to introduce to you our president and our beloved Pope. Please be seated, because tonight I have the pleasure and the honor to present to you a person of importance. The situation tonight is different than the other night. I ask you to pay attention, concentrate on everything that is said. I would ask you to refrain from clapping and talking. And now, let me introduce to you Mr. Gianni Masi."

Despite the secretary's request, there was a short, conservative round of applause. I got up and walked toward the podium. "Thank you. Thank you very much. Monsignor the Pope, Mr. President, ladies and gentlemen: I thank you, because you give me a grand opportunity to be here and to speak with you. And I thank you for taking the time to listen to my message, for it is of great importance for the future of our planet."

Before I continued the story, I introduced myself again and summarized what I had told them the night before.

Chapter Eleven

After finishing the summary, I paused. "Before I go on," I said, "I want to ask you if you have any questions regarding what I said last night."

A number of people rose to ask questions. I called on one in the second row.

"Your story is different than others," he said, "but the beginning of your story is similar to others. That is not too surprising. Can you explain why?"

"Yes," I said, "the Strangers have come here many, many times over thousands of years in search of the truth. Most of the time their visits were in vain. That is why nobody knew about them. They never left behind any trace of their presence. That is why we have had no proof of them until now. What happened to me is the same as of what you read in other people's accounts. But my story has one distinct difference, because now I have evidence of what occurred to me. That is why this story will change everything forever."

Someone toward the back of the room, a professor of astronomy, exclaimed, "I hope that you have proof of what you are saying and what happened to you! What I have read and heard of other alien encounters never provides any proof. There is no hard evidence for the existence of any visitors. The only thing we know is the false information about the Roswell, New Mexico, UFO incident in 1957, misleading information put out by the United States' government."

"Ladies and gentlemen," I continued, "again tonight you will witness the truth. I hope by seeing the proof that I have you will be convinced that these Strangers exist. I am the only one who can prove their existence to you without any doubt and beyond any question." At this, everyone grew silent. "All this will occur in the future. I don't know what year or century it will be because in the future they don't measure time in months, years, and centuries like we do on Earth. To me, it seemed like a long time into the future. But like I said, they are very different from us. The world there is so different. It looks like a paradise, calm and tranquil. They are all united; there is no conflict. It was so relaxing and calm that I had a hard time even thinking about returning to my world. But I needed to return because if I stayed, the past, the present, and the future would suffer some major consequences. When I was there and observed the way they lived and the way they controlled their world without government or laws, it was very hard for me to understand, because in this world we have to have all kinds of different laws. And our lives are full of imperfections. Our problem here in this world is that we are defective. And the way we understand nature is flawed. We ourselves, we have a limited intelligence. We want to be powerful without power. We want to be virtuous without virtue. We want to be superior without superiority. That is why we have a lot of misunderstandings and wars. We are a creation without control, and yet we try so desperately to control everything. We like to control by force. Our love is not deep. We have a lot of evil in our hearts. Instead of helping one another, we neglect each other, because we enjoy seeing the other suffer pain and fear."

I look at them, and I saw their faces with their eyes wide open. What I had said surprised and stupefied them. But I continued, undeterred.

"The world there is very different. There is no hate or envy. The most magnificent thing is that they all govern their world together. After I witnessed their world, how it was and how they maintained order, it was almost impossible for me to understand. Our chances here in our world, the planet Earth … we have no hope for the future. It is an ugly world. What you saw and what you are going to see will begin sometime in the twenty-first century, our future. We will have an end to our lives and the planet earth. Before I tell you how it will happen, I want to tell you that the end will not occur because of the Strangers or what you would call them, aliens. We are going to accomplish this ourselves.

"The Strangers have the capacity of destroying our world or other planets if they choose to. They could even destroy galaxies. Not only can they destroy, but they can also create. If they wanted to destroy this planet, our planet earth, they would have done this a long time ago. The Strangers are not destructive and for this we need to thank God! If they do choose to come here, they could come here right now to our meeting; they are right here right now."

When I said that, they all stood up and turned around. They looked at each other with a frightened feeling. Finally, one of the high ranking generals got up and asked me a question. "What are you saying? Are you saying that these aliens have the capability of destroying us all? Including this planet? How? How? With nuclear bombs? Or laser beams? What kind of energy do they posses? It must be something incredible to destroy a planet. How do they travel to come here? What kind of spaceship do they have? What kind of transportation? I would like to know? Is it like a big military mission? If I understand correctly, they can travel at the speed of light. If they possess this kind of knowledge and power, even if we united the armies of the world, we would not be effective against them. Right?"

"Yes," I replied. "If the Strangers were destructive beings, this world would have no hope for salvation. You couldn't escape from their power; the world would be consumed. Fortunately, they have no intention of conquering or destroying this world or any other. These beings are peaceful. They are very distressed by the way we live and the way we treat our planet. To answer your question about their mode of transportation, they do have ways to go the speed of light. They don't have any gasoline or any mechanical instrumentation. Their means of travel get formed according to their needs, where they are going and what type of speed they require. They have everything necessary. Everything is prepared automatically. They don't have a military. They don't need anything like that. Each one of them is responsible for what they do.

They don't have nuclear bombs or laser power. They do have some type of energy that again I can't explain to you because I don't understand it myself. We don't have that capability."

The general continued his line of questioning. "I would like to ask how they defend themselves from intruders or enemies"

"Like I said before, they have no enemies."

"So then tell me," the general demanded, "how can they destroy planets or galaxies like you just told us if they don't have any military and no nuclear power or and lasers. I am really curious to know."

"The simply eliminate and materialize any way they want to," I said calmly. "For them it is easy. With their telekinetic power, they can control any type of energy. Anything that the universe provides they can use for their needs. They can make electricity or magnetism. They use all the power of nature from any planet they are near. They use gases and any type of liquid for energy. It is an advanced intelligence, and we could never understand it or have any possibility of using it."

Chapter Twelve

I continued with my answer. "If we want to defend ourselves against them, our power is of a minimum standard, but we don't need to worry about that. The problem that we have is ourselves, because we are destructive race. I know, because the Strangers showed me both our past and our future.

Another person stood up and introduced himself as a scientist. He said, "Those in my field are working very hard to develop ways to improve our quality of life. We are engaged in the study of magnetism and the strength of nature. We are working to develop some kind of travel instrument that will allow us to approach the speed of light. At this point we have no conclusive answers. We understand clearly that humans are destructive and we know we are destroying our planet. My question is, what we can do to engage in something more effective and desirable?"

"The problem is this," I said. "We humans like to build things and then destroy them. The history of the human race is nothing to be proud of. From the beginning, we did horrendous things, killing and destroying again and again. This will continue until the end of the world. In our history, we have accomplished a lot of good thing. We changed the lives of many people for the better. We invented some good things to help our race. But the destructive inventions are much more common in our history.

I paused for a second to collect my thoughts. "The things that I saw with the Strangers began with the beginning of the world. Like I told you, before the beginning of the world everything was peaceful and beautiful. But somehow something changed. I couldn't determine what it was. Year after year the human race became more destructive, and for everything that we invented, people found ways to use it for destruction. The evil overcame the good. Human life became complicated. I was seeing things that were hard for me to understand. Being a human being myself, I couldn't believe what I was seeing."

I was interrupted by someone who stood up and introduced herself as a doctor. "I am the head of Milano Family Hospital," she began. "Sir, I would like to ask you what kind of medicine they practice there. Do they have doctors? How do they cure the people there? What kind of hospitals do they have? Are they like ours, or are they much different? What kind of medical schools do they have? How do they begin to comprehend diseases, plagues, and other phenomena that we have here on earth? Can you explain this to me, please?" She thanked me and sat back down.

"It is very easy to respond. Being a doctor, you would know that the human race has problems with diseases. Finding a cure for all of them is almost impossible. Hospitals are full these days. Our bodies are very vulnerable to germs, microbes, and virus of any kind, and that's why we have more problems. But as for the Strangers, they don't have doctors or hospitals or medicine. They don't have any diseases or plagues like we do. If anything like that occurs, they have the capacity for self-curing with their mental capability. The capacity of their brains is so vibrant and full of energy that there is no limit to what they can do. In a word, they have no doctors because they do not need them."

Another person asked about their personal lives. "What do they do among themselves? What do they eat? To be so healthy and in great shape, like you said, what kind of exercises do they do to maintain this fantastic form? How can they be so disciplined? As a follow up question, I wanted to know whether you saw any births there."

I smiled, remembering the happy groups of people I had seen among the Strangers. "First of all, there is a lot to do. One beautiful thing that you can do there is play with all the animals. Or you could dive underwater and move down to the deep without swimming or even worry about oxygen tanks. At the same time, you can fly in the air without airplanes. The most precious thing is to travel with your family and just enjoy the world. This is what they do there for fun. As for eating, they do eat fruits and vegetables, and they drink water. The fruits, vegetables, and water are much different than here. They are all pure, and everything is so delicious. They don't have wine, beer, or any kind of liquor. Neither do they eat meat, including fish and birds.

To answer your question in regards of birth, yes I

witnessed a woman giving birth. She was not in pain or uncomfortable in any way. There it is one woman for a man and one man for a woman. The women there have the capacity for only three births. After that they are not able to have any more babies. They are genetically engineered this way. They have children at a very young age. They have the three babies in their youth, as soon as they reach puberty. They are ready physically and mentally. When they have their babies, they use their mind to control the whole body. The body will have all that is necessary to sustain the mother and her child. They don't need to do any labor or exercise.

"I also want to tell you the quality of their physical appearance. They all are in great shape. The male is about two meters ten centimeters tall, with a weight of about one hundred thirty-five kilograms. He can alter his weight from one hundred and thirty five kilograms to an unlimited weight. They use the pressure of gravity and all the energy of planets and the universe to contort themselves. Other than that, they look just like us. They have white skin and white teeth. They have perfect facial features with light blue eyes and wavy black hair. The females are beautiful. They all look like models. They are tall, about one meter ninety-five centimeters. Their body weight is about seventy-five kilograms. They can alter their weight just like the males from seventy-five kilograms to an unlimited weight. They also have white skin with blue eyes and black wavy hair. The females have long hair. They don't use makeup or anything to alter their looks. They don't have to. They are already perfect."

Perfection

The people there respect one another. They don't glorify one another, and they don't have hate. They also don't betray one another, and they don't know what gossip is. They live in peace without any bad thoughts or feelings."

After I said all that to them, they looked at me with a silent and mesmerized look. Then all of a sudden, I noticed that many people in the audience had nervous grins on their faces. From the back, I heard someone say "huh?" Another person stood up and addressed me. "What a fantastic way of living! They have no diseases, sickness, or worries about anything. It is a perfect life. They have no envy, jealousy, or hate. It seems like an impossible dream. Every single one of us would love a life like that, with love and tranquility. For us it is just in our dreams. We don't have this type of life. Maybe it is because we are bad people with bad ideas as you say, or maybe it has some other cause. But to have a life like them, we would need to begin again, with a new life, a new birth." He paused for a moment, then asked, "But is it too late for our race?"

While he stood there in thought, another person, closer to the front, got up and said, "Mr. Gianni, why did they send you back? Why didn't they come with you, so that they could talk to us and explain these things to the world?"

"Excuse me," I said. "I would like to know who you are. Could you please introduce yourself?"

"Yes, of course," he said. "I am the head of administration for the Italian government."

"Mr. Administrator, if they came here with me, if you

91

and the rest of the people of this planet saw them, you would not know what to do with these Strangers. It would be a shock to you and everyone else. The problem would be that you, as an administrator, would have no control over how the population would react toward them. Another problem is that they can't live here with us. They cannot walk around like us. They don't breathe our air. Planet Earth is contaminated. With the curiosity and suspicion that we have in our nature, the first thing that we would do is take them prisoner. We would study them to understand who they are, how they live, and where they come from. You know that we would do this not to know them but to learn their powers so that we could use them to our own advantage. My friends, they know how difficult it would be for us to communicate face-to-face.

"As to your second question, they chose me because my bloodline is closely connected with their own. I know; I know; that sounds a bit artificial, but I know that in a few moments this will all be clear to you. That is why I came back to explain it to you. The danger that we are facing is a future without the human race. They sent me with a message, so we will be informed. We have to deal with this situation slowly. We need people with intelligence to accomplish certain things, especially in the fields of science and medicine, particularly the field of genetic engineering. These Strangers need to know every step we have made in genetic engineering. The future holds much danger for our planet, the human race, and our universe. The Strangers know that there is something in space that is very dark and evil, with a destructive mind."

Chapter Thirteen

I paused, allowing my words to sink in. The worried expressions on the faces of everyone there reassured me that they were taking my message seriously. I continued. "The Strangers know of these different creatures; they feel they will destroy the earth. They are coming to our future, which is the Strangers' past. These aliens want to destroy us and the Strangers. When the evil beings arrive here in our time, they are going to make us suffer worse than animals. They will use the human race for their own gain.

"My reason for coming here is to talk to all of you and to find the truth. We need to work hard to uncover the truth, the truth of these Strangers and these evil beings. There is more, much more to say, but for now ladies and gentlemen I will stop. There will be a lot more to come."

Before I could return to my seat, one other person asked me a question. "Excuse me, what kind of proof is this? You are just telling us stories. It seems to me to be nothing, only another story from someone with a rich imagination. It is like fiction with no proof whatsoever."

While this person was asking me these questions, a noise like the wind suddenly passed through the hall, followed by a noise like thunder. The lights went out, and I could sense the tension from everyone in the room. The ball the Strangers gave me moved. It flew to the back of the room. It changed from a dark, opaque color, becoming clear like the daylight. It was much brighter than before. As we watched, the ball began to grow. It was getting larger. Then the ball began to go around the room, and finally came to rest, hovering in the middle of the room. It began spinning rapidly and changing colors from red to blue to green, flashing like a bright kaleidoscope. Finally, it became crystal clear, like water. The shape of a face began to take form in the ball, and soon I recognized the face of the Stranger. The ball spun to face me.

"Thank you very much, dear Gianni," the Stranger said. "Now we will take over. We will explain everything that we need to explain to them."

I saw the faces of the people in the room. They appeared paralyzed. They did not know what was going on or what would happen. They were hypnotized by the Stranger's face. The ball that turned to the face of the Stranger started to spin, becoming a three dimensional image of the Stranger's face all around the room. The face was looking at everything and everyone. The people became terrified and confused. Chaos ensued when they all tried to get out of the room. It was clear they were panicking. But a soft voice came from the ball to calm them down, and it had an immediate effect. They all sat down, and for a moment it was quite silent. They were staring at the face and waiting. After a few second the soft voice spoke.

Chapter Fourteen

"Friends," the Stranger said, "I thank you very much for coming here tonight, and for paying attention to all that my friend Gianni said. We thank you for being patient with him. He is a very important person to us, because without him this meeting would never have taken place. I beg you to be seated and be comfortable. Please just listen, because what I have to tell you is very important to you in our past and for us in your future. I will tell you everything. After I finish, Gianni will have for you one last word, and after that we will go. We hope everything that Gianni told you is clear in your minds. We know that you have a lot of questions about us. What are we? Where do we come from? How can this be possible? Who created us? And, perhaps most pressing to your minds, what agenda do we have? All this will be explained to you in time. For now we travel to the past so that you can see what we need you to do."

The ball spun again and the face of the Stranger disappeared. The color changed rapidly, finally settling on blues and greens, colors that moved into position to form a view of the earth. The people in the room were hypnotized. They looked at this magnificent ball as if the planet Earth were inside this room. Then the ball began to show the story of the human race from the beginning to the end. It was just like I had seen when I was over with the Strangers. The ball showed them everything I had seen and more. The picture was so intense; it was extraordinary. They showed in a fraction of time a little section about me and my visit with them. At this point, what was going on was like short stories, showing pieces and bits of the accomplishments of the human race. The ball displayed beautiful human creations and cities. They showed the accomplishments of mechanical invention and the capability of flying. They showed all kinds of ships, cars, and all kinds of vehicles. They were going back and forth, showing the invention of communication networks and satellites.

Then the ball stopped for a few seconds and returned to resembling the earth. Then it showed old laboratories where people were studying all types of medicine and all types of cures. It showed all types of buildings around the world. The ball arrived to a point of the most terrible invention that human kind could develop: the atomic bomb. In a split second, the ball showed a test of this incredible invention. The ball changed to resemble an atomic explosion in the center of the room. It was frightening. The room became dark and the ball turned to the planet Earth again. It was peaceful, quiet, and tranquil for a moment, and then the ball showed bits and pieces of World War II. It was an intense scene of battles in Europe, including a lot of dead people. But the most deaths came with the dropping of the two atomic bombs.

As they saw the sign that the Stranger was giving them, they were unable to comprehend it all. They saw everything, but were confused. They reacted with fear and shock. They looked at each other as though they were seeing the future.

I tried to reassure them. "Please be calm," I said. "Relax and be seated. Everything that you saw will happen, but for now you can't worry because you need to understand what is going on here first. It is for your own good, because if you don't understand you will panic and get confused."

The people observed the destruction of the world, minute by minute. They saw the end of creation, but they also saw the beginning of creation. They saw paradise from the beginning after Adam. He was beautiful and perfect. He was relaxed and tranquil with all of the animals and vegetation. Everything was green with flowers of all colors and qualities. There were rivers lakes and oceans. Millions of birds and animals. Everything was perfect. They saw the beginning of humanity. They saw exactly the same thing that I saw, but in a different way. Then everything changed. The ball again engaged into a new demonstration. In a few minutes the ball showed just some of the accomplishments of humanity, both good and bad. Then in a flash it showed them a major world war with all its destruction. The most incredible thing that I saw with those people was the invention of cloning. These new studies, called genetic engineering, cloned all types of things, from plants to all different types of animals. Then slowly they tested human DNA. All of this was against nature. So the ball changed from showing the cloning to displaying the future. The ball showed a spaceship taking off from Earth to test a new experiment, the human experiment.

That was the trip of no return. After this the ball became blue, then red like blood. It showed the planet earth covered in flames. What was happening was the end of the planet, the end of the world. After the red faded, it was dark in the room, until suddenly everything turned blue. The people looked again, and the ball had become planet earth. Its form then returned to the face of the Stranger, and the room became illuminated. Everyone looked at the face of the Stranger with many questions.

With a deep and calm voice, the Stranger announced, "What you saw is a fact of the human race that is not so appealing, and your end is arriving fast. Soon there will be no human race. There is nothing you can do to stop it. Only one thing could stop this, and that is to travel into the past and to begin a just and righteous way of life. But for you it is impossible; you don't have the ability to travel into the past. If we do this traveling to the past and change the past for you, then we change human history. We change your way of life; we change the planet's life, and eventually we would harm ourselves in the future. Because of this, we will not interfere with your history. What we want to know is this: our race is white, but here in the past you have great diversity in the human race. People of all colors. You have white, black, and brown. You have all types of features that we don't have in the future. What we don't understand is what happened in space. What happened when the space ship took off from earth to study genetic engineering, DNA, and cloning?

"What kind of sacrifice did you have to make for this genetic engineering medical study? Why use only people of my kind? Why were other kinds of people, like Africans, Asians, South Americans, and all the other races that you have in this world of the past not included? We would like an answer from you. If you don't have an answer, then we need to change your future so that we can maintain our world. You need to find an answer as rapidly as possible."

A professor spoke up. "Pardon me! What is it that you want to know? What kind of answer do you expect from us? The way you are talking, you are speaking of the future, and we here in the present don't know what will happen in our future."

"We need to know what happened in space," the Stranger replied. "We know pretty much everything else, but we have a blind spot as to what happened between the middle period of the research and our creation. We would like to know what happened during that particular time. We are in the dark about this. It is the only thing we don't know about our history. We have no knowledge of whether anything bad happened there in space."

Another professor of science responded to the Stranger's statement. "What are you trying to say to us? That we will do something disastrous? That we will disturb the nature of the world?

"Not only will you disturb your world," the Stranger said, "but also the universe. Because of this we need to know exactly what happened during the time for which we have no records."

A doctor joined the discussion. "Are you saying that we will disturb human nature? That we will use science and medicine to produce a new race?"

"Yes," the Stranger replied. "It is a very dangerous project, and it will not be done correctly. This will destroy the past world and the future world."

At this the Pope rose. Everyone else immediately became silent. He addressed the Stranger in a grave tone of voice. "You that come here from the future, you know our destiny. You can change it for good, right? But to do all of this, you will disturb nature as it is. You will be disturbing God's creation, and this can destroy the human race! Where do you put God in all of this?"

The Stranger did not respond immediately. He seemed to be trying to decide how to respond. Finally, he merely asked, "What is God? I don't understand."

"God is the creator of heaven and Earth," the Pope said. "God created our world and the entire universe that you know, including humans, animals, and plants."

The Stranger smiled. "Who created us? Humans did, right? You! And we created our new world. We don't know or recognize this creator called 'God.' We learned nothing of significance of this from our ancestors. We know that we came from space. Our creation was among the stars. We also know that you humans worship many of what you call 'gods'."

Chapter Fifteen

A doctor of genetic engineering asked the Stranger, "What is it that you want us to do? How can we help you—and ourselves—understand what will happen in the future? How can we fill in all that is missing in your knowledge of what happened on that spaceship? We have no way of knowing what will happen to us or to you in the future."

"You need to get together with everyone that you can possibly find," the Stranger said. "You need to locate people who know science and medicine. You need people who study history and writers that can make a difference. You must bring together all kinds of scholars who have done studies in medicine and science and genetic engineering. We need doctors with knowledge of genes and DNA to find out what is going on in the future, because at this time we don't have the ability to discover what will happen in the future. This is the beginning of the twenty-first century, but all that will occur will take place far away in the future."

The Italian president said, "I have a question. Why are you communicating with us here in Italy but not with people in other countries?"

"The answer is simple," the Stranger replied. "We

circled the earth for many years, present and future. In the future—our present—we found no record concerning what happened aboard the spaceship. There is no information whatsoever about our creation, no samples of our DNA. That is why we are here at this particular time. This is your present and our past. Here we see a different life, somewhat advanced but with different qualities and methods for creating things. But most importantly, we found here a trace of our DNA. We found an ancestor in our bloodline: Gianni."

At this, half of the people seated stood up and exclaimed, "Gianni!" All eyes were turned on me. The Italian president asked the people to remain calm and be seated. He asked the Stranger for an explanation. The people sat down, but they continued to look at me. I could see fear on some of their faces.

Then the ball changed. It started to show virtual scenes. It showed a multitude of people from the past and the future. It was all people I knew. I saw my father, my grandfather, and ancestors going back many generations. They were all of the same race. All were white. All were attractive. Then the ball showed me as an adult. Then the images disappeared and the ball took the form of the Stranger's face again.

One of the professors who had asked a question earlier continued to look at me, but he addressed the Stranger. "This generation is only of the line of Gianni? I am a history professor, but I see nothing special about this line. This family plays no special role in our history. Why was this genetic line chosen?"

"We don't know why he was chosen," the Stranger said, "but we do know that we were infused with genetic material from his descendants."

Then a doctor asked a question. "From what I understand of all of this, you want to know about our medicine and science, but for the moment we are only beginning to understand how to do genetic engineering, let alone cloning. You have told us it happens in the future. If you have the ability to do genetic engineering, why don't you give us that information so that we can understand what we need to do? At least let us know where we need to go for research to find some answers."

"As I said before," the Stranger replied, "to understand what will occur in the future, you need to find your most knowledgeable people. We need doctors of medicine and science and professors of history. That will be your first step. If we don't begin with this, everything will be in vain. Before something terrible occurs, such as the end of your world, we need to discover the truth of this matter." With that, the Stranger finished. He said goodbye to everyone and disappeared into nothing. The ball became crystal clear before it also disappeared.

All of the people in the hall wore an expression of incredulity. They were waiting for the next instructions or for more information.

After a few moments of their stunned silence, I said, "Ladies and gentlemen, from this moment forth, we need is to follow the Stranger's instructions and as soon as possible. We must start today!"

The Search

I indicated to the president that the meeting could be adjourned and asked him to tell everybody to find people qualified for this quest. The president walked slowly to the podium, apparently deep in thought.

"Before we adjourn," he said, "I would like to say that I will be in contact with the presidents of Britain, France, Russia, and the United States to inform them of the situation and request that they contribute scholars and scientists to this endeavor. When we gather again, the entire world will be involved. It will be the first time the entire planet has joined together to work toward a single goal."

After the president spoke and gave everyone instructions, the group was adjourned. Some people left immediately, while others stayed, huddle together in small groups, discussing what they had just been told and how to move forward.

They took with them all that they had seen and witnessed. With great haste, they began to search for the best people available in science, medicine, and research. They brought together people of invention and mechanics. They got people of mathematics, geography, and astronomy. Slowly, small groups were getting together in different parts of the world. They had all been told that the Strangers would come back to evaluate their work with the hopes of finding the truth.

Ten days went passed. These groups began to converge on Rome for a unified conference. At the insistence of the Pope, they met at the Vatican. The Pope, of course, was present at all sessions, as was the president of Italy. Scientists and scholars from all over the world attended. It was exactly like the Strangers advised them to do. The presidents of almost every country attended as well. It was as if the United Nations was meeting in Italy, except now the nations were truly united by a common cause. Italy took the lead in this matter, since we had been the ones contacted by the Strangers.

When everyone was assembled, the first plenary session was held. The Italian president stood up and walked toward the podium. "Your holiness, gathered leaders of all nations, ladies and gentlemen," he began. "First of all I would like to thank you for coming here today. Our purpose for being here is of the greatest importance, and I am pleased that all nations have come together to work toward this common goal. We would like to begin as soon as possible to search for an answer before it is too late. If you have any questions, please ask them now."

The president of Russia rose. Speaking through a translator, he said, "I don't understand what all of this represents. I am puzzled. I need an explanation."

"Yes, you have the right to know everything that is going on," the president of Italy said.

"The same goes for me," said the Chinese president. "I would like to know everything in regards to this situation. To me, the reports we have received seem exaggerated. I hope I am not wasting my time in this place today."

"I certainly understand your hesitancy and confusion," the Italian President continued. "But you will see everything that is necessary for you to understand. I have no doubt you will find it as convincing as we did."

At this point, the president of the United States rose. "This story you have told us, the information you have shared … this seems more like science fiction, UFO stories fit for cheap magazines. Do you have any evidence to back your claims? I don't want just words. I would like to know the facts as soon as possible."

Chapter Sixteen

The Italian president tried to calm the assembly. "I know. Like I said before, you need proof. Without proof everything is in vain."

"I am sure of this," the Pope said. "I pray and hope that our God will help us with all of this, because we definitely need major, major help."

After all the arguments, all the questions and answers, the Italian president said, "Before we go on with this, I would like to introduce to all of you someone that some of you already know. He is a very important person. You can ask him all of the questions that you wish. Ladies and gentlemen, again I will introduce you to our friend, Gianni."

I stood up and approached the podium as the people applauded. "Thank you," I began. "You are very kind. I just want to tell you a few things in regards to this situation." They looked at each other. I could tell many of them had serious doubts. "You need proof so that all of this can be valid, but the proof that you need is not from me. It is from the Strangers."

After that I felt a strange vibration. I saw that little ball fly out of my bag toward the center of the Vatican. There it became larger. The lights in the room went out, leaving everything dark like the night. Then the ball began to form images. The whole room was engulfed in this darkness, and it looked like the universe with billions of stars and galaxies. Then a planet appeared, followed by other planets. It looked like we were moving at the speed of light from planet to planet. Slowly, our visual voyage came to our galaxy. It passed through the outer planets in our solar system. The image went through the sun and through the moon. It approached the earth and entered our atmosphere. Then everything disappeared, and the ball took the form of the Stranger's face.

The Stranger Departed

The face appeared in a different form than it had before. It was covered with the same silver chrome material that covers their bodies. In a moment, everything was calm. Then the Stranger spoke.

"This is the last time that you will see me. We would like to know what you have been able to discover in regards to the spaceship and cloning. What we want to know is the truth: what happened in your future, the beginning of our creation? We need information about our creation. Did you look at all the documents available to you? Did you find out when the study of genetic engineering commenced? And why? If you don't have an answer in a few days, we know that your planet, Earth, and the human race will be destroyed. So you know that it is important to find an answer. We can work together to save this planet and this world. We feel that when you began our creation, you also created another, and we suspect the other creation is malicious. We feel a disturbance of energy around us. It is created by this malicious entity. They are going around the universe in search of their creator. As we travel from past to future and through galaxies, we feel this energy, full of darkness and malice. We will not take any questions at this time. You need to go to work in search of the answer. Gianni will be the bridge of communication between us and you. Anything that you need to say, any questions you have need to go through him."

At this, the Stranger disappeared from that room, and the lighting returned to its normal level. Some people stood up and looked around the room for him, but the Stranger was gone.

"Please," I said. "All of you be seated and listen to what I have to say."

They took their seats, but many of them continued to talk. A lot of them asked questions at the same time. "Where did he go? Where did he disappear to? Is he still here? What are they going to do? Are they going to find the answer themselves? All of this is so confusing. It seems like a game of UFO."

I tried once again to calm them. "Can you please stay seated and quiet down a little bit, or I will just go! Yes, something will happen here. First of all, go find everything that is necessary to discover what happened from the beginning and what will occur in the future about their creation. Find the truth in regards to genetic engineering and cloning, before it is too late. Please just get going because this matter is very important. It is more important than your own lives."

One by one they got up and took off to find all of the necessary documentation of this agenda. At the same time, the Strangers were above the planet Earth, over the atmosphere, circling the planet from north to south and from east to west like guardians of the universe.

As people were leaving, the Italian president announced, "Before everyone goes, I would like to have a meeting to discuss this situation with all of the presidents of each country, as well as the generals of the united forces.

A general stood up and asked a question. "If all of this is true, we need to prepare our military forces. We need to unite all of the military power of the world and prepare a defense."

"I think that the general is right," said the president of Russia.

The president of United States stood up. He paused for a moment, then said, "I have to think about this because this conflict could become a nuclear war or even—God forbid!—a war in space."

The president of China added, "We will do anything necessary for the protection of our people and our world."

The prime minister of Great Britain was next to speak. "The situation seems a bit bad. We need to step back and consider whether this could all be made up. It seems to me that we shouldn't take it too seriously, because if we prepare ourselves militarily, it could lead to a catastrophe. Not to mention the fact that it would be very expensive."

The French president agreed. "I think we need to be calm. Before we react, we need to find out everything we possibly can in regards to this situation. My colleague from Britain is right; it could be very costly."

All the presidents reached an accord to begin searching for any and all information concerning genetic engineering that could lead to cloning. They agreed to meet again, this time in the United States. The president invited the world leaders to meet at the White House. Twelve days went by. Communication continued among the leaders of the world and the scientists who met to discuss their discoveries.

In space the Strangers departed after many years of circling the planet and searching our galaxy without any success. In our time, our scientists made a few advances in genetic engineering, but not enough to answer the Strangers' questions. Everything they needed to know happened in our future, somewhere between fifty and a hundred years from now. We were simply unable to discover the future.

Six months passed and with no luck. During that time, I had no communication with the leaders, and the Strangers had not contacted me again.

Discovery after discovery was made. Things began to change on Earth. Science advanced; life became even more complicated; and many years went by. Slowly we approached the point in time when the Strangers said we would build a spaceship. By that point, I had grown old. I was eighty years old, and my wife, Anna, was seventy-six years old. Our children had long since grown up, gotten married, and had children of their own.

It was around this time that they created the new spaceship. It was launched into space, with many scientists and doctors aboard. Their mission was one of research. They were charged with developing significant advanced scientific studies. They remained in space for about two years, after which time they briefly returned to earth. Not long after, they returned to space for their second and most complete study of genetic engineering. Now they were working on vegetables, plants, and animals. These initial experiments were a success. It seemed that everything went well, so they continued and expanded their studies above the earth. They worked toward dramatic advances in genetic engineering, eventually moving to using human DNA in their experiments.

In the five years following the beginning of the second mission, many things were occurring in our world. Many bad things. The economy crashed. Diseases spread. Famine and war were worldwide. Europe became the most power-ful government in the world. They called for a united world order. The participants in the united world order were Europe, Russia, and the United States. They controlled the economy and all of the business in the world. The rich became richer, while the poor were under the control of the mighty power. The situation deteriorated to the point that a world-wide revolution occurred. The world became a dark, unpleasant, and evil place to live. Three years went by and Gianni died. With this everything changed for the human race because it changed for the Strangers. About five years later the spaceship traveled into the universe far away from the planet earth. There they finally discovered the secret of cloning. At home on the planet Earth, a world war began. It was the biggest ever.

It began with explosions everywhere. There was destruction of enormous magnitude throughout the world. Little by little, the planet was burning. The Strangers had no knowledge of this happening because Gianni was dead. The next time the Strangers came to the Earth, the planet was consumed by fire. They had no idea what happened. But they knew they needed to travel through the galaxy forever. They must be vigilant, making sure there was no one out there in the universe that could destroy their green planet. Because that new planet where the Strangers lived was Earth. The Strangers had renewed it after finding it in ruins.

Chapter Seventeen

The search continued for eternity for the Strangers. The Strangers couldn't live without worries, because their lives depended on what happened in that spaceship before their creation. They believed—or more precisely, they sensed—that there is some malice somewhere in the universe. They didn't have an idea how bad the other creation was. They didn't know what form it took, where it drew its power, or how destructive its mind was. But they knew that it was a species that could not only disturb the Strangers' planet and disrupt their tranquility but could also destroy other planets. So the Strangers remained the guardians of the universe and all the galaxies it contained.

Not too far from the galaxy to which the earth belongs, something terrible is traveling at the speed of light, coming toward the earth with a roar of terror. Is this what the Strangers fear? Is this the real UFO? Are these the aliens that we fear? Will this be an encounter of the fourth kind? And if it is, what kind of power do they have?

To be continued.

Epilogue

In conclusion, we arrive at the end of this book. As I explained in the beginning, in regards to UFO stories, we have no proof. UFOs can be of any kind. Just put yourself in an imagined situation, and you can come up with any stories about UFOs. This is my story. It is not that it is true, but it is possible, especially if we are not careful about what we do. If we don't take responsibility for the topics we study and the things we invent for the betterment of the human race, that is, if we don't take moral responsibility for what we do today, we shall pay the consequences of tomorrow. Every advance in our knowledge of electronics, machinery, equipment, science, and medicine can be dangerous, because humans have no limits on the things they are able to do. Because humans are not satisfied with today's accomplishments, we feel the need to come up with new ideas and inventions for tomorrow. Man is not happy with himself. He needs to go forth with technology. He becomes infused with ideas, and discovery becomes a disease of the mind. Humans need to do powerful things because they are directing themselves to become gods. But there is a problem: humans are imperfect in everything we do. We will self-destruct. Man will never become a god. Our ability to create is from God. God set limits to our creativity, and when the limit is exceeded, humanity is terminated. Because of its situation, humanity is complicated. The complication is a life of lies, and with lies nothing is clear. The lie becomes bigger. The more man lies the bigger the lie becomes. It reaches a point of no return, and then the lies will blow up in to bigger and bigger imagination. Then it is all done for the human race. This is how I understand UFOs, the way I see life, and the way I believe in God. God is truth the truth can't be change.

ooooo

Thanks to my Lord Jesus Christ for the knowledge and for my life in this world. All good accomplishments are because of Him, my God.

I am dedicating this book to my mother, Gaetana Masi (1922–1969). She will be in my heart for eternity.

I would like to thank my family.

Special thanks to Christopher Pascucci for the computer stenograph.

I would like to thank you for buying this book, and I hope you enjoyed it. Look for my next and most intriguing book in the near future.

What is this?

CPSIA information can be obtained at www.ICGtesting.com
Printed in the USA
BVOW010114120713

325391BV00008B/93/P

9 781450 707794